GW00374190

Published by Margin Notes Books, 2010

First published by Heinemann, 1931

British Library Cataloging in Publication Data
A catalogue record for this book is available from the British Library

Printed in Great Britain by the MPG Books Group, Bodmin and King's Lynn

ISBN 978-0-9564626-0-2

www.marginnotesbooks.com

Published by Margin Notes Books
5 White Oak Square
London Road
Swanley
Kent BR8 7AG

The Whicharts

by Noel Streatfeild

Margin Notes Books

CHAPTER 1

The Whichart children lived in the Cromwell Road. At that end of it which is furthest away from the Brompton Road, and yet sufficiently near it to be taken to look at the dolls' houses in the Victoria and Albert every wet day, and if not too wet expected to "save the penny and walk."

Saving the penny and walking was a great feature of their childhood.

"Our Father," Maimie the eldest would say, "must have been a definitely taxi person; he couldn't have known about walking, or he'd never have bought a house at the far end of the longest road in London."

"Our Father," Tania the second child would argue, "was a Rolls-Royce man, his own you know, I don't believe he ever hired anything."

Their Father was a legendary hero to the children. They knew so little about him, and that little sounded so exciting. "Our Father would have done this, or said that", they would romance. No story was too improbable for such a man.

He had been a soldier, with many honours, and even more mistresses. His first mistress, or at least the one credited with being his first, was a Miss Rose Howard. She belonged to a most rigidly respectable family, and was at that time twenty-two.

She met the Brigadier, as she always called him, at a military ball. He was a Captain in those days, and newly married to a lady of such remarkable social eminence and blue blood, that he was guaranteed a brilliant future. He saw Rose, and fell in love. With the Brigadier to be in love was to make love. This he did entrancingly. So entrancingly that he persuaded Rose to leave her family, her home, her respectability, to live in the Cromwell Road under his guardianship.

Followed months of quarrels and frictions with her family. Outraged fathers, uncles, brothers, cousins, strode wrathfully down the Cromwell Road, and savagely rang her bell. Ten minutes later, these same outraged fathers, brothers, uncles, cousins, strode even more wrathfully up the Cromwell Road. Either having rung her bell in vain, or seen such a glowing and happy Rose, that their showers of angry words were not only unable to hurt her, but seemed scarcely to reach her understanding. Finally they held a meeting. No women were present, Rose and her affairs were not fit for a woman's ears. She had long been nothing but a scandalised whisper in the family, now she was to cease to be even a whisper. She had chosen a life of shame, then let her live it. Her family never wished to see or hear of her again.

Joyously Rose told this news to her Brigadier. "How perfect," she breathed in his ear, "we're all alone in the world now, fancy never seeing or hearing any of them again."

"Fancy, darling," echoed the Brigadier. But he looked pensive.

Grace, the Brigadier's wife, bore his lapse from fidelity with well-bred indifference. Generations during which her family had found fewer and fewer people, "Really fit to know, my dear!" had reduced their marriageable circle to smaller and smaller dimensions, until at last they had been forced to marry each other. The Brigadier was one of the few members of the family, brought in from outside, as it were, perhaps in the hope of improving the stock. For this rather internal system of marriage had produced in Grace a something which in a more plebeian circle would have been described as "a brick loose," but in her own family was described as, "Grace is so reposeful, dear thing, nothing seems to move her." Certain it is that she was utterly unconcerned by this the first, or any subsequent affair that "Deah George," as she called him, walked or fell into. So Rose was free to enjoy her Brigadier in the Cromwell Road to her heart's content.

Perhaps the fact that Rose was all alone in the world except for himself. Perhaps her love, such a very undemanding love, touched him. But he stuck to Rose longer than to any of the other women in his life. He was with her for eight years. Of course during those eight years there may have been moments, backslidings, but the fact remains that for eight years he was an almost daily visitor in the Cromwell Road.

One day he told her that he wasn't coming back. He had always said if she should tire of him or he of her, they must at once tell each other the truth. To Rose the contingency had been too awful to contemplate, and her side of the bargain simply a joke.

"Tire of him!" Heavens above! how could anyone tire of such a man.

It was a wet afternoon in November. The streets looked like grey ice. On the tops of the buses unlucky people who couldn't squeeze inside huddled under the mackintosh covers. Wet dogs half walked and half were blown down the road. The lamps were just being lit, and their little yellow glow picked out the slanting grey lead pencils of rain. A truly deplorable November day. Rose had been staring rather gloomily out of the window. She thought the Brigadier had been strange lately, hadn't made love to her. True, that was no novelty, he'd always been like that, crazy about her one minute, crushing her, unable to leave her alone, then suddenly full of casual talk of people and things, scarcely a kiss when he arrived, and when he left. But this was different, now he was—what was he? She wouldn't confess it even to herself, but wasn't there a something? The door opened, and he hurried in.

Courage was a thing the Brigadier never lacked. He told her at once. There was someone else. Maimie. Daughter of a Scotch minister. It was all terribly difficult. Her family would kill him if they knew, but there it was, they adored one another.

"Oh Rose, she's so lovely. She's a selfish little devil. She'll never be to me one half what you have been. But I can't resist her. Can't see life without her".

After a time he left her. He explained a lot first. It seemed she was to have enough to live on. The house was hers. Oh, a lot more. Somehow she couldn't hear clearly. He said he'd write. Then the front door slammed.

Ever afterwards when she saw from that window

the pavements wet with rain she would find herself straining to hear the front door slam.

She never knew what she did that winter. She supposed she ate and drank and lived as usual, for when the spring came she was still alive, at least her body moved. Then suddenly in April she was ill. Nothing much, influenza, but it seemed as though she would never get better, no will to live, nothing to get up for, a perfectly blank grey future.

People won't let you die. The doctor and nurses collected by the frightened cook and housemaid, dragged her unwilling spirit back to earth. Carted her protesting body to Brighton. And in the early autumn returned her more or less intact to the Cromwell Road.

During all these months Rose had no word from the Brigadier. True, she always had news of him from the papers. He was always in the papers. News of someone you love that you learn through the papers is worse than no news at all. Rose soon learnt that.

In October he turned up again.

The bell rang. His footsteps sounded on the stairs exactly as though ten and a half tortured months had not gone by since she had heard them last. In he walked. Told Rose she looked a bit peaky. Hoped she wasn't doing too much.

"You women never know when to stop, burn the candle both ends, out all day and all night."

Rose, living for the first time after ten and a half dead months, vaguely agreed.

"I say, old lady," he blundered on, "I wonder if

you'd do me a great favour?"

Maimie, it seemed, was going to have a baby.

"You've no idea," he explained, "just how awful it is. Her people are Scots, and narrow-minded. My God! Rose, you've no idea how narrow-minded, would call what we've been doing fornication! Maimie's got caught —daren't go home, poor little devil, and well——"

Out it came. Would Rose take her in?—just till the baby was born—they'd find someone nice to adopt it—Maimie could make excuses to her family—they wouldn't like it of course,—but they'd never come south—they'd never find out.

"If Maimie's here, he will come here," thought Rose. But all she said was, "Bring Maimie to me."

That was a funny winter. Rose often looked back and smiled at the memory of it. Maimie and she had so little in common, and yet she'd grown fond of the girl, who could help it? Maimie was a magnificent creature, tall, fair, with big blue eyes, and the most winning personality. People couldn't help adoring her. Everyone in Rose's household adored her. The housemaid who thought she was steering straight for Hell's fires. Nannie who came a month before the baby was born, learnt the truth, and said she'd leave that night, and stayed for the rest of her life. The doctor who on a cold December morning brought the little Maimie into the world. "Look," he said, "here's a lovely daughter for you," and was deeply hurt to hear the mother say, "Oh, take the little horror away! Thank God somebody's going to adopt it." But he still worshipped Maimie.

Rose watched Maimie in the days that followed for a sign that she cared even a little for her baby. There was none. The girl was unfeignedly thankful that a ghastly worry was nearly over. She wanted nothing but to know that the baby was safely adopted, and herself in the train on the way to Scotland and respectability.

"But your baby. Can't you see, Maimie, some day you'll want her, you'll wonder where she is, you'll miss her, my dear, it isn't natural what you're doing. Women were meant to be mothers."

"If you feel like that keep her yourself. A reputation's a wretched thing to lose. Before the year is out I shall be married—well married—then I mean to have a wonderful time, but until then, no—once bitten, my dear! What kind of a life would I have with that tied on to me," she would point a disgusted finger at the baby, "you must be mad to suggest it!"

One day the Brigadier came to them in triumph. He'd found a splendid couple to adopt little Maimie.

"Cheer up, old lady, it will all be over soon; we shall be out of the wood, we shall never hear of the poor little devil again."

Rose was not a maternal woman, but little Maimie's fate touched her. There must be something of the Brigadier in the baby. It didn't show, but it must be there.

"Don't have her adopted," she said, "I'll keep her."

Before Maimie left Rose produced a Bible.

"Laugh if you like, but your baby has got to have something to remember you by. I want you to give her this Bible. Sign your name and address here."

Maimie glared at the blank fly-leaf, then she turned to Rose.

"You must be mad! Here am I moving heaven and earth to hide what I've done, and you ask me to give myself away. Leave the child my name and address? I should never feel safe for a moment. Why, she could use it against me at any time."

Rose looked at her.

"Can't you trust me? I swear as long as I live she shall never have this book, and when I am dead she shall only have it if she's grown up the sort of person one"—she hesitated—"one can trust to use it discreetly," she finished lamely.

Months of being hopelessly miserable had brought Rose strength of character. She hadn't exactly hardened, but she had grown to a woman. Two years before she could not have persuaded Maimie into saying good-morning, against her will. Now she made her sign the Bible.

"To little Maimie," she wrote in her dashing hand. She wrote her name in full, and added the address.

"Thank you." Rose locked away the book. "You can trust me."

Little Maimie settled down in the Cromwell Road. She had a nursery at the top of the house. Rose was sweet to her. Nannie worshipped her. Cook petted her, and was sorry for her. To the housemaid she was a figure of romance.

Then one spring day when she was nearly one-and-a-half the Brigadier turned up again.

He did not come alone. He brought Tania.

She was the daughter of an extremely wealthy newspaper magnate. He had married a Russian of slightly royal blood. The result was Tania.

She was crushed but still proud.

Yes, she'd been an inconceivable idiot. "Imagine it —going to have a baby—I've had plenty of men before—how could I have been so careless—God knows!—however, there it is—yes, next month positively boresome!"

Rose took the Brigadier into another room.

"This is getting past a joke; I'm not the Queen Charlotte. I'll take in Tania, I like her, but she is the last. You can have all the Bettys, and Doris's, and Flossies you like, but no one else shall have a baby here."

The Brigadier was hurt.

"You're getting the teeniest bit hard. You used to be such a soft little thing. Don't let things make you hard, old lady. Such a pity. Nothing in life is worth it."

Rose looked at him. She couldn't think of anything to say.

She loved Tania. She was charming. All moods. Up in the clouds one minute, down in the depths the next. She had blue eyes, the Russian high cheek-bones, and shining black hair. She had inherited her father's quick business brain. From her mother a love of the arts. Music, pictures, a piece of good acting, all brought a quick sighing gasp of pleasure. But she was incapable of expressing herself. All she would say was, "Deevy!" or "Too quaint."

She was a trouble to look after. Had never done a thing for herself in her life. In some way ordinary things, such as turning on her bath, or mending her own clothes, hurt her. She said nothing, never complained or asked for help. But a curious flush would rise under her skin, and her whole body express resentment at a world which could expect such commonplaces of her.

She was a never-ending source of amusement to Rose. Neither of the servants nor Nannie cared for her as they had for Maimie. But they respected her, and treated her as though she were married.

She was very ill when her baby was born. Her bones were so small. She endured agony for hours. She never moaned. Rose looked in once, and was horrified at the girl's white tortured face. Tania smiled at her. "Positively too painsome," she whispered.

Tania's baby was also a girl. Little Tania. There was no talk this time of adoption. There was Nannie, there was the nursery. Rose, too, was by that time so fond of the girl she was glad to keep her baby.

The night before Tania left Rose produced a Bible.

"She shan't ever have it during my life," she explained. "But I like to think that perhaps some day, years and years ahead, she could find you if she really needed you. I made Maimie sign one too."

There was a pause. Then Tania's head dropped on the book. Her sobs grated through the room.

"I can't, Rose, I can't; I've tried, but I can't give my baby up."

She was over-persuaded by the Brigadier.

"You can't ruin your life, old lady, what chance have you with a baby? None. Leave her to Rose."

The next day she went away. The last glimpse Rose ever had of her was a drooping figure in the corner of a taxi. A white face tried to smile at her, it was a gallant effort, but undeceiving. All happiness seemed to have left her.

Nannie, who was a philosopher, accepted the second baby cheerfully.

"Very nice for Maimie to 'ave a companion."

After the blue eyes and golden curls of Maimie, she considered the new arrival's dark eyes and sallow skin a tragedy.

"It's easy to see who's goin' to be Miss Plain in this nursery," she said.

CHAPTER 2

A year later the war started. At first it meant
nothing to Rose. Rather exciting perhaps. Broke
the monotony. Something to talk about. Then
suddenly she found she was wanted. She had lived in a
trance since that November day when the Brigadier
had left her. Nothing to get up for in the mornings.
Nothing to do all day. She couldn't even feel the
babies needed her, she was their guardian, but Nannie
was their life. Now with the war she was wanted again.

A woman she knew asked her to help at an
equipment office. Troops, it seemed, were camped
everywhere, and there weren't enough mattresses—
palliasses they called them. Rose agreed at once. She
understood sewing-machines, she didn't mind scraping
all the skin off her fingers tearing up ticking. She
worked for hours at a stretch. Very much wanted.
Making new friends every minute. Really happy.

Such few friends as she possessed had known her
history, and had taken her, and her nursery for granted.
These new friends presented a difficulty. She wanted
to ask them to the Cromwell Road for a hurried
meal—between palliasses, so to speak. But the babies!

She tackled Nannie. "How shall I explain them?"

"Well, Miss, you've nothing to 'ide—they aren't
yours, though that's what people will say—and that's
'ard on you, and 'ard on them—if I was you I should
think of a good lie and stick to it."

"Yes," said Rose. "I will".

"Now who are they?" she puzzled. "Orphans? No, on the whole not orphans, they take such a lot of explaining. 'What! both parents dead! Poor little dears, do tell me how it happened,' No, decidedly not orphans." She couldn't face that. "Parents abroad? Yes, that was better." Parents abroad only live in one place—India.

She went in search of Nannie. "I'm looking after the babies while their parents are in India."

"And very nice too, many of the best children 'as their parents abroad."

"Would you explain all this to Cook and Annie for me, we must all say the same?"

"You leave 'em to me, Miss," Nannie replied grimly.

As it happened, Rose wasn't called upon for further invention. The babies were admired. The story of India believed. The women who came in and out were always in a rush. In those early war days everyone was far too busy and important to ask questions about babies, unless they happened to be Belgian refugees.

In the summer of 1915 the Brigadier turned up. He was a most conspicuous and important figure. The papers were full of him. He was worried and anxious. His eyes looked tired.

"You know, Rose, one never knows what's going to happen these days—a lot of my money was in shows abroad—I'm damned poor now—but you'll be all right—I've seen a lawyer about you—this house is yours—you can do what you like with it—leave it where you like—and there's enough money settled on you to bring in about five hundred a year whatever happens to me."

"And the babies?"

That was the trouble. The money he had settled on her was all he had to settle. The rest was tied up on Grace. Of course as long as he lived he would see they were all right. Send money as usual. But if anything should happen to him, she'd have to get someone to adopt the children.

Rose questioned him about himself. Gently probed to see if Tania still held the field.

He looked ashamed. He'd left poor Tania.

"Took it terribly hard, poor little devil—didn't seem to understand that you can't force love—when it's dead it's dead."

The was there someone else?

The Brigadier's face lit up. His eyes ceased to be tired. He'd fallen in love, he said, as he'd never fallen before.

"Imagine it, Rose—me a staid old soldier—and I've fallen for a golden-haired dancer—I might be a subaltern."

The golden-haired dancer was apparently called Daisy. She lived in Balham. Just got her first part. Had always been in the chorus before.

"By Jove! Rose, that girl can dance."

He didn't get much leave now, but all he could scrounge he spent with Daisy.

"You two must meet some day—you'd love each other."

Rose went up to the nursery. She picked up baby

18

Tania and sat her on her knee. Afterwards Nannie told Cook she had never before seen Miss Howard take such an interest in Tania.

She couldn't know that somehow Rose hoped to comfort the mother by loving the baby.

One night early in 1916 the door bell rang. Cook answered it. Money had been so scarce lately that Annie had been dispensed with.

Afterwards describing the scene to Nannie, Cook would say:

"And there 'e stood, but that white and queer-looking I declare to you I didn't know 'im. 'e'd a bundle in 'is arms. 'Fetch Miss 'oward quick,' 'e says to me all of a gasp like. And I runs for Miss 'oward. Down the stairs she comes like a streak. Looks in 'is face. 'Oh my dear,' she says all lovin' like, 'what is it? 'oo's 'urt you?' 'It's Daisy,' 'e says, 'she's dead, and she's left me this'. 'e pulls back the shawl from the bundle in 'is arms. And believe me or believe me not, there lay a baby girl. 'Cook,' says Miss 'oward, all as casual as though babies came to our 'ouse every day———"

"Which in a manner of speaking they do," Nannie would interrupt.

" 'Take this baby up to the nursery, and give 'er to Nannie. Tell 'er I'll explain later.' With that she pops Daisy here in me arms. Leads the gentleman into the drawing-room. And shuts the door."

Poor Brigadier. Life had caught him at last.

Hurrying home to spend his few days' leave with his Daisy, he arrived to find her dead.

19

Her father had told him just what he thought of him, and had pushed the baby into his arms. "Take her. She's yours. Our Daisy was everything to us, you've killed her. We don't want any brat of yours about the place to remind us of you."

The Brigadier went back to France.

"Come and see me off, Rose. I've a sort of feeling this is the end. I shan't come back."

Rose arrived at Victoria in the early hours of the morning. It was dreary and cold. The station was shrouded in grey mist. On the platform everyone was cheerful, with that dreadful smile that is entirely an action of the mouth, and can be continued however large the lump in the throat. Mothers chatted to their sons. Wives to their husbands. Sisters to their brothers. All curiously restrained. Grown-up boys going back to a school they didn't care about—nothing more.

The Brigadier arrived late.

"Bless you, Rose. God bless you, my dear. Good-bye."

He got into the train. It slowly steamed away. She turned to go. Her eyes were full of tears. She couldn't see properly and bumped into a girl. She murmured her apologies. But the girl didn't hear, she seemed frozen, staring at the bend where she had last seen the train. Suddenly she grew conscious of Rose, she tried to speak, but only a cracked whisper came.

Rose never knew what the girl had said. But that morning in Victoria Station she understood war.

CHAPTER 3

The sudden appearance of little Daisy caused a slight fracas in the nursery.

On the evening of her arrival, after the Brigadier had left, Rose had gone up to examine the baby.

She found its little crumpled red body lying face downwards on Nannie's flannel-aproned knee. Nannie, holding an enormous powder-puff, looked up as Rose came in.

"I was 'opin' you'd come up, Miss. This is too much, this is."

She angrily shook a shower of "Fuller's Earth" on Daisy's underneath.

"I know, Nannie, but what can I do? Here she is."

Rose looked helplessly at Daisy.

"'Tisn't right. 'Ere are we, Maimie four-and-a-'alf. Tania nearly three. Old enough as you might say to know what's what. And suddenly down you pops this little fly-by-night come by God knows 'ow. 'Taint right."

"Oh, but Nannie, they're half-sisters."

"And 'oo's the Mother? That's what I likes to know in my nursery. Miss Anybody for all we knows."

"I believe she was a dancer."

"So I should say."

Nannie snorted in disgust.

"Just the sort of Mother I should expect. Blessed lamb!" she added to the baby.

Rose was worried.

"After all," she said, "the other mothers were——"

Nannie interrupted.

"As nice a pair of young ladies as you could wish. If unfortunate. If I lives to be a hundred I'll always speak well of Miss Maimie. Speak as you find I say. As for Miss Tania: well, she was quite the little lady. As I often says to Cook, it was 'ard to believe she 'adn't got no wedding-ring. And now this! A dancer indeed!"

Nannie bristling with indignation pulled a tiny vest over Daisy's unprotesting little head.

"Well, Nannie, if that's how you feel, she must go."

"Go! 'oo said go? She's come, an' she must stay. But she starts with a nasty 'andicap, po'r little thin'. An' there's one thing I do say: come by as she's been, let's start 'er decent. Christened she must be to-morrow mornin'. It didn't so much matter for the others leavin' it a week or two. But one startin' life as this one starts, you can't be too careful."

Rose got to her feet.

"Right, Nannie. I'll arrange for it first thing to-morrow morning. And you must be godmother."

This was a stroke of genius. The last words Rose heard as she shut the door were:

"Godmother indeed. Blessed lamb!"

The summer of 1916 passed peaceably over the Cromwell Road. Rose worked hard at her equipment office. The babies cooed and quarrelled in the nursery.

But money was growing short.

"I must find paid work in the autumn," Rose thought.

Before the autumn the Brigadier died.

He died, according to the papers, from pneumonia. Actually it was from exhaustion; he had been terribly overworked. Perhaps too he wasn't very anxious to live.

His death was on every tongue. His face on every placard.

Rose sent for Nannie and Cook.

"Both of you have been with me so long, that you know the secrets in this house. Maimie is now five, and very quick——"

"Sharp as a needle," agreed Cook.

"I don't want the children ever to know who their father was. If they ask you awkward questions please just say that he was a soldier".

"And died for 'is country like a 'ero," added Nannie.

Rose smiled sadly.

"Yes, you can say that if you like. Only never his name. You understand, don't you?"

The death of the Brigadier made Rose feel curiously isolated. It was as though the *raison d'etre* of her life had gone. She cared. But more as a spectator than as the person to whom something had happened. His leaving her, had happened so long ago. His leaving the earth couldn't take him further from her.

Money grew really scarce. The Brigadier's shares had fallen. The five hundred a year he had settled on Rose proved to be a doubtful four.

Rose looked round for paid work, and instantly thought of munitions. Fabulous stories were abroad as to what women earned in munitions.

"If others can do it, why not me?" she thought.

She got a job gauging in a fuse factory. The gaugers

were not as well paid as the women who worked the lathes, but they sat for their work. As they worked in shifts of twelve hours, Rose knew her earning days would be short if she was expected to stand.

She worked from seven in the morning until seven at night for a fortnight. Then reversed, and worked at seven at night until seven in the morning.

She went to work on a workmen's train. And whether working by night, or working by day, returned so tired that she had time for nothing but to fall thankfully into the bath Nannie had ready for her. And to eat quite unconsciously any food set before her.

She struggled daily with thousands of other workers through a police-guarded gate. She had a numbered disc, which checked her time-keeping. She wore a dreary khaki apron and cap. She became with the passing months almost an automaton. The ferrules of millions of fuses passed through her fingers. She gauged them all, and either rejected them or passed them on.

There were pleasant little pauses in the work. The ten minutes that was on day-shift breakfast, and on night-shift tea. The hour for dinner. The half-hour for tea on day-shift, and breakfast on night.

There were curious long nights when her eyelids seemed to weigh a ton. Nothing would keep them open. When she would start back from the depths of sleep as the overseer banged a hammer on the table.

There was the roar, roar, roar, of the thousand lathes. The curious smell of hot brass. The queer hootings outside from strange little engines. A hooting which when she heard it in after-days, always brought back the war.

The nights when there were air-raids. The sudden bray of the warning hooter. The curious silence that followed, as the power was turned off, and the straps stood still.

The hurrying and running with everyone else to get under the concrete roof. The half-hour of waiting that followed. The distant booming of the guns, nearer and nearer. The smashing sound as pieces from the anti-aircraft shells fell through the glass roof. The chitter-chatter of the machine-guns. The pause as the enemy passed on to central London. The feeling of cold and exhaustion now that the excitement was over. The terror of falling asleep in case the rats ran over you. The distant booming beginning again. The enemy passing overhead. The half-hour wait. Then up with the lights. The roar, roar, roar of the straps. Cold and exhausted back to work.

She stood it for a year, and then was caught by the influenza epidemic. Coming in from work one day, she fainted in the hall.

Nannie, in spite of three babies, nursed her wonderfully. But she was quite ill. And it was a fortnight before she really sat up, and paid attention to life. Then it was the thought of the money she was missing that pulled her together.

"Nannie," she said, "I must get back to work on Monday."

"We'll see," Nannie humoured her.

"We won't do anything of the kind, it's a case of

must. I've been having a doctor and medicine. Where's the money coming from?"

Nannie sat down on the end of the bed.

"It's time you an' me 'ad a talk," she said.

Nannie, it seemed, in the proud position of friend of the mothers of two of the babies, and godmother to the third baby, considered herself in a position to dictate about the future.

"Things needs lookin' into. Maimie's nearly six, and sharp as a cartload of monkeys. Tania's four. There's Daisy on me 'ands, me nurseries to do, and what time I 'as left for givin' a 'and to Cook. It can't go on. Cook can't do all the 'ouse alone, and it's time Maimie 'ad a bit of teachin', and it wouldn't do Tania no 'arm neither. I've taught 'em their prayers, an' that's about all. The children's ignorant, an' the 'ouse downright dirty. Now what? 'Let!' says Cook. And let! says I. 'ere's all the 'otels full, 'ere's 'alf the 'ouse empty. Take in a nice couple. Or two young ladies. Or even two gents. Give 'em bedsitting-rooms on the second floor, where your bedroom and the spare bedroom is now. And send Maimie an' Tania to school. That leaves me free so I can give a 'and to Cook. An' out of what the lodgers pays 'ave a woman in now an' then to 'elp with the cleanin' an' that."

"School?" Rose looked thoughtful. "Aren't schools terribly expensive?"

"They are, an' they aren't, so to speak. An' you've no cause to be flyin' 'igh. I've found a very nice school not far from 'ere. Very moderate it is. An' very nice little children I seen go in an' out."

Rose was impressed.

"Well, Nannie, you have been looking about. Do you think perhaps Daisy could go to school too, or is she too young?"

Nannie snorted with indignation.

"Maybe with your munitions, an' your illness an' that, you're forgettin'. Daisy's one year an' eight months. No school would take 'er at that age. Per'aps, Miss, you thought of sending the blessed lamb to a crèche?"

"Of course not, Nannie; how dreadful of me. I never remember their ages."

Rose did not go back to the factory for a month. During that time she found two girls to take her rooms.

They were friends, working for the Y.M.C.A. They had been living in great discomfort in a hostel, and were delighted with the Cromwell Road. Rose also examined the school. It was not the class of school she had been at herself. But she was charmed with the headmistress. The education was very thorough—terrifyingly so, Rose thought. She spoke vaguely of the children as her wards, and said she might send them to the kindergarten next term.

In the nursery Rose confided a difficulty to Nannie.

"If we send the babies to school, what are we going to call them?"

Maimie was standing by the window. She turned round and came to Rose.

"At school, Howdy, they will call us by our name."

All the babies called Rose "Howdy." It was a relic

27

of the older Maimie. It avoided the usual "Aunt." In that house it was a mistake to stress imaginary relationships.

Rose put her arm round Maimie.

"What name, darling?"

Tania's little sallow face looked up at Rose from her other knee. She had a curious fastidious aloofness. So very like her mother, Rose often thought. Now the child stood by her, but wouldn't touch her.

"By our Faver's name in course."

Rose was puzzled.

"What name, darling?"

"Whichart, in course."

Rose must have looked hopelessly fogged, because Maimie said kindly as one helping an imbecile:

"Our Father Whichart."

"In Heaven, you know," Tania added.

Rose looked helplessly at Nannie, who for once was nonplussed. But Maimie continued firmly:

"Everybody takes their Father's name. Cook told me so. So I'm Maimie Whichart. And Tania's Tania Whichart. And that——."

She pointed a scornful finger at the youthful Daisy, who was crawling rapidly across the nursery floor.

"That is Daisy Whichart."

Rose looked at Nannie.

"Out of the mouths of babes," she murmured.

CHAPTER 4

Maimie and Tania went to the kindergarten. At once Nannie found herself in difficulties.

Maimie asked:

"Have me an' Tania a pension? I expect we must have. There's lots of children at our school whose fathers were killed in the war, and they all has pensions."

"So 'ave you, no doubt."

Nannie carefully felt her ground.

"That'll be what Miss 'oward pays for your schoolin' with."

A day or two later Maimie asked:

"Are we orphans? They asked me that in school, an' I said I thought my mother died when I was a teeny weeny baby, 'cos I'd never seen her. And Miss Jones laughed an' said she thought I'd got that wrong somehow 'cos I'd got two younger sisters. When did our mother die?"

Nannie fell weakly back on an old slogan of the nursery:

"Them 'as asks no questions, won't be told no lies," she said severely.

"Which means 'as you don't know," Maimie retorted.

That night when the tired Rose had bathed, and was eating her dinner in bed, Nannie came in.

"Can I have a few words with you, Miss?"

Nannie poured forth her tale of woe.

"An' what was I to say? Maimie's no fool, you can't put 'er off all any'ow like you could a year ago. It's my belief the only way is to tell them the truth."

Rose was horrified.

"Surely not, Nannie. What can little children understand of such things?"

"Little children isn't what they was. And neither Maimie nor Tania's ordinary children neither," Nannie added proudly.

On the following Sunday Rose decided to have a talk with the children.

She was in bed. She sent for Maimie and Tania, who scrambled up beside her. They were full of conversation, and told her about their school. Maimie said she was very backward.

"Imagine it, Howdy. Other children as old as me have read and written for years, and years, an' years, an' here's me six an' nearly two months an' can't read a word."

Tania joined in:

"Yes, an' me an' Maimie in one form, there isn't anyone else as big as Maimie in our form."

Maimie said:

"Miss Jones said she never did see two sisters so unlike, an' I said she should see Daisy as she's unliker still."

"I like Miss Jones," Tania added, "she called me 'Brown Eyed Sue', an' she asked me where I got my black hair from. But I didn't say nothing, 'cos I didn't know."

Maimie broke in:

"Silly! You was borned with it in course. Wasn't she, Howdy?"

"Miss Jones meant," Rose explained, "did you get it from your father or your mother."

"An' which did I?" asked Tania, interested at once.

"From your mother, darling. You are all much more like your mothers than your father."

Rose carefully accented the plural, but neither child noticed.

"But you have your father's eyes, Tania."

"Oh, Howdy!" Maimie exclaimed, "that does remind me. Are we orphants? I asked Nannie, but she's silly; she doesn't know. Are we?"

Rose decided that the moment had come.

"I want you both to be very big grown-up girls, and try and understand what I'm going to tell you.

She told them their history rather as though it was a fairy-story. Unconsciously she painted the Brigadier in vivid colours. He sounded like a fairy prince.

The mothers were more difficult. Neither child would allow one mother to possess something the other didn't.

Rose said:

"Your mother was very musical, Tania. Perhaps you will be some day."

Maimie burst in:

"Mine was very musical too, I remember perfec'ly, played everything. Pianos, violins, drums, harps, barrel-organs, just everything."

"Your mother was a very lovely person," Rose

laughed. "You have very much her colouring. Maybe you'll grow as tall as she was. She was very tall indeed."

"My mother," said Tania gravely, "was a giantess. She was so tall she knocked her hat off on the trees. I remember perfic'ly."

"She wasn't a giantess at all. Tania's telling stories, isn't she, Howdy?"

Maimie beat the bed to gain Rose's attention

"I'm the eldest, so I must have had the best mother, mustn't I?"

Rose hushed them.

"Listen, darlings, you both had lovely mothers. I cared for them both. But this is what you've got to understand. Having a mother each isn't usual for sisters. I don't want you to feel unusual, or other people to think you unusual. So, except to Nannie, or to me, I don't want you ever to speak of your mothers. Just say you are orphans and——"

"Our father was a great soldier, an' died like a hero," Maimie interrupted.

Rose smiled. Nannie had taught her lesson well.

"Run away now, darlings, I'm going to sleep."

The children ran out. Two seconds later the door opened again. Maimie poked in her head.

"Howdy," she asked in a hoarse whisper, "did Daisy ever have a mother?"

Rose laughed.

"Why, yes, of course she did. Everyone has a mother. I never knew Daisy's. I was told she had been a dancer, and lived at Balham."

"I think," Maimie said, as she shut the door, "Daisy

looks the sort of person whose mother you wouldn't know."

Their mothers as a topic for conversation interested the children for a very short time. For with the excitement of school, they soon drifted into the background.

Once Tania said:

"Betty Smith asked me why I hadn't no mother. An' I said it was a secret an' I mustn't tell nobody."

Nannie sighed. She couldn't feel that Rose had helped the situation much.

That autumn the war ended. Rose, after so many months of such strenuous work, felt like a watch must feel when its mainspring snaps.

Even on the day the Armistice was signed, she was incapable of going mad with the rest of the world. Nannie went mad. The babies, waving flags, had a holiday, and went mad too. Cook for the first time in her life got roaring drunk.

But for Rose the Armistice merely represented new difficulties. Of course she was glad it was over. That the awful fighting had stopped. But she would lose her job. Men would be demobilised by thousands. They would all want work. Rose had no particular talent. She was trained for nothing. The house was hers. But there were the three children to dress, and feed, and educate. Nannie and Cook to feed, and their wages to pay. And herself to dress and feed. And all to come out of four hundred a year. She must get advice. She must ask a man. Men understood money.

She wrote to the Brigadier's lawyers, through whom

she received her income. They made an appointment to see her.

Rose had never realised until she stood on the doorstep of the stupendously grand offices of Messrs. Bray, Hopkins and Bray, exactly how cheap she would feel. It was so long since she had been the Brigadier's mistress. And during those years when she had been, she had been so cut adrift from the disapproving, that "living in sin" had become as it were natural to her. She had really felt quite good. Very like a wife must feel.

But as her feet sank deeper and deeper into the pile carpets of Messrs. Bray, Hopkins and Bray, she suddenly realised what an outcast she was. For to the Brigadier's lawyers, she must simply be the late Brigadier's mistress. It was they who had bought her house in the Cromwell Road, and later legally tied it up on her. It was they who quarter by quarter sent her allowance, addressed in large type to Miss! Howard. No! it was no good trying to present an innocent front to Messrs. Bray, Hopkins and Bray.

"Young Mr. Bray" saw her. "Young Mr. Bray" was about sixty. Rose wondered as she looked at his grey hairs and bent back how old "Old Mr. Bray" could be. She knew there must be an old Mr. Bray, for the clerk who had shown in had said "Young Mr. Bray" would see her, as Mr. Bray was busy with an important client, and could not be disturbed. Rose, flustered, had stammered, "Oh anybody, Mr Hopkins would do." The clerk had eyed her severely and said that "Mr Hopkins had been dead these many years."

At first "Young Mr. Bray" did nothing to put Rose at her ease. He talked to her rather as though they were both at a funeral, and she the corpse. He spoke in hushed tones of one in the presence of the dead. Looking timidly at the vast files in the shelves, she wondered that he spoke to her at all. For his life, judging by the names on the files, had been spent exclusively with the great, the powerful, and the illustrious.

"No wonder he makes me feel as though I were dead," thought Rose humbly. "How wretched for him to have to waste his time on me."

But if "Young Mr. Bray" treated her like a corpse, his questions were skilful.

Rose had merely meant to ask him if there was any way by which the Brigadier's four hundred could become five hundred again. But before she knew where she was she had told him all her story. Her life with the Brigadier. The arrivals of Maimie, Tania, and Daisy. The munitions ending. All her worries.

Then suddenly, and for no reason that Rose could see, "Young Mr Bray" ceased attending a funeral. He lit a cigarette, and became rather like a father. Not like Rose's own shocked and outraged father, but like a most kind, helpful, and understanding father.

She stayed over an hour. In that time they planned to turn most of the house into furnished rooms. To herself assist Cook with the housework, instead of looking for a job outside. And before she left, she promised "Young Mr. Bray" that whatever difficulties she had, she would always come and discuss them with him.

As she reached the street, Rose found her eyes blinded with unexpected tears.

"May I say," "Young Mr. Bray" had said, "that I have the very deepest admiration for you, Miss Howard."

The spring of 1919 found Rose living in a bed-sitting-room. And three sets of boarders, all with bedrooms and sitting rooms, living in the house.

They managed very well, for Daisy was now three, and old enough to trot after Nannie clutching a duster and brush. She was, as Nannie proudly said, "A rare one about a house." No longer tied to her nursery, Nannie could help Rose and Cook. "Young Mr. Bray's" scheme worked very well.

The Williams' lived on the ground floor. A very nervy and irritable ex-officer and his young wife. He was looking for work. Meanwhile he lived on his gratuity. Rose hoped he would find a job quickly. Because his gratuity wouldn't last for ever, and she could not see herself turning them out.

On the second floor she kept the two friends, who were still wanted by the Y.M.C.A.

The third floor was taken by a dancing-mistress. Nannie didn't think much of the third floor, who was pretty, but a little painted.

"Not quite our class. Let's 'ope she pays regular. Looks easy come, easy go to me."

"Oh Nannie," Rose scolded, "don't be so uncharitable, she looks a nice little thing."

"Excuse me, Miss, you're no one to judge, what

your 'ead's full of 's 'eart."

The third floor was called Violet Grimshaw. She was a never-ending source of joy to the children, because she possessed a gramophone. The nursery toys were very simple things, presents for birthdays and at Christmas given by Nannie, Rose and Cook. They had never before had a gramophone in the house. Maimie and Daisy clamoured for it every time they saw Violet. Tania, though fond of music, seldom came in to listen; she never willingly went into the boarder's rooms.

She explained this to Rose.

"I do hate all these strange persons about our house. It doesn't feel as if it was our house at all."

Rose secretly agreed. But she said:

"We are really very lucky to have them, darling. But for them you'd have no new clothes, and perhaps hardly enough to eat."

Tania replied gravely:

"In course I know, Howdy, that it's got to be, but I hates it just the same."

Violet tried to teach Maimie to dance. She would put a dance record on her gramophone, and show the child simple steps. While Daisy sat on the floor and watched.

One day Daisy insisted on dancing too. With much vigour, her flat little white shoes bobbing up and down, her red curls jigging with her, she gave a reasonably correct performance of the steps she had seen Maimie learning.

"Bless me!" Violet exclaimed, "I believe Daisy's

going to make a dancer."

She watched the child for some weeks. Carefully teaching her easy little steps and exercises. Then she went to Rose.

"I say! I know you have a bit of a job to make both ends meet. I see a way by which the children might help. I believe Daisy has the makings of a dancer. And Maimie's not only lovely, but a graceful little thing. I don't know whether she'll be any good, but she could do troupe work. Tania I've never seen dance because she won't come inside my door, but she's got an ear for music, she hangs about outside if ever I play any of my highbrow stuff. Now what I suggest, dear, is that you let me introduce you to Madame Elise."

She looked expectantly at Rose, who looked quite blank.

"Surely you've heard of Madame Elise, dear? Taught hundreds of dancers. Taught me! You send the kids to her, and in panto, and off and on, they could earn a bit to help. Not yet of course, they're too young for a licence. After all the kids aren't yours, why not let them learn to help themselves."

"Oh, I couldn't," Rose said. "Poor babies, I should hate them to feel they had to earn anything yet. Time enough when they're grown up."

Rose told Nannie of Violet's suggestion. She expected it to be greeted with snorts of rage. To her amazement Nannie rather took to the idea.

"It's no good not facin' fac's. Earn their own livin's they'll 'ave to, an' the sooner the better. I looks at Maimie sometimes, an' I says to myself it's to be 'oped she marries young, for fitted for anythin' else she won't be! She don't work at 'er books. She 'ates 'ousework. She's already thinkin' a deal too much of that pretty face of 'ers. But I shouldn't wonder if she could do the dancin'. As she'll 'ave to earn 'er livin' the stage might suit 'er fine."

"It's Daisy who seems to have the talent," said Rose.

"Blessed lamb! Takes after 'er mother, I suppose," Nannie spoke unbelievingly.

"What about Tania? If the other two learn, she may as well. Do you think she'll like the stage, Nannie?"

"She's a funny one she is, spittin' image of 'er mother. You remember 'ow proud 'er mother was, 'ow she 'ated admittin' what was comin' to 'er? If it 'adn't been as it was plain as a pike-staff 'alf a mile away, she would never 'ave said a word, but 'ave 'ad 'er baby all casual-like, in a 'edge as like as not! That's 'ow it is with Tania. She may 'ave a pain, but she never says so. I 'ave to watch that child like a cat watchin' a mouse, or I'd never know 'ow she was. It's the same with people, she's that fond of Maimie, but she never shows it. But if Maimie says a rough word to 'er she turns as white as a sheet, but never a word. Life's comin' 'ard on 'er anyways. If the others learn the dancin' she may as well."

"Nannie approves of your suggestion," Rose said to Violet, "and anything Nannie approves of happens in this house. So will you take me to see Madame What's-her-name?"

Three days later Rose found herself climbing innumerable stone stairs, to where, on the top floor, a large wooden board proclaimed the fact that Madame Elise had an academy of dancing. They reached a dusty hall, hung with dozens of weather-beaten posters of pantomimes and music-halls, in which the offspring of "The Madame Elise Academy" had appeared. There were "Madame Elise's Little Wonders." And "Madame Elise's Dancing Dots" and "Madame Elise's Children's Ballet." And, "The children appearing in this pantomime are Madame Elise's Wonder Mites."

"Does well, doesn't she?" said Violet, giving an admiring nod at the posters.

They came into a small and incredibly dusty office. The walls were apparently a pale dirty green, but were practically invisible, owing to the array of photographs with which they were covered. Some were large groups, evidently of pantomimes, and showed Madame Elise's pupils in every variety of pantomime dress. There were children's pierrot troupes, and groups from different ballets. Also large signed photographs of apparently star performers, for they had printed slips stuck on the frames, saying, "Kiddy Kathie." Or "Little Doris, the Child Wonder." Or "Bubbles, of the Madame Elise Babies' Ballet". Each photograph signed in a round childish hand, "From Kathie, Doris, or Bubbles, to dear Madame."

Rose had scarcely time to get her breath, for such a galaxy of infant marvels startled her, when the door opened and Madame Elise hurried in.

She was a strange scraggy figure. She looked as

though when melted she had been poured into a dress of black velvet and allowed to set there. For it was obvious that never under any circumstance could that dress come off. Such black velvet, so coated and overlaid with the dust of years, that in some lights it appeared grey, and in others brown. She had a white face, and should have had white eyelashes and eyebrows. But when she remembered, and without ever looking in the looking-glass, she painted on reddish-brown eyebrows, coal-black lashes, and a scarlet gash for a mouth. All these additions to her beauty owing to lack of time and looking-glass, slightly out of the straight, which gave her a curiously rakish air. On top of all this she wore a bright red wig. A wig which years before may have been brushed and dressed, but which obviously, since it became the property of Madame Elise, had been popped on without a brush or a comb ever going near it. She was a tall woman. In the studio she diminished her height by wearing pink cotton ballet shoes, in the street she wore buff kid button boots.

One thing she possessed that no curiosities of appearance could hide. A pair of very lovely and amazingly shrewd, kindly blue eyes.

Violet explained about the children.

"Where are they? Where are they? Where are they? Must see them. Must see them. Must see them."

Every time Rose met Madame, she was struck afresh by this curious habit of repeating everything three times.

Violet explained. She spoke of the children as

Rose's wards. She said she thought she had discovered a hopeful child in the youngest. Might Rose see the pupils at their work? Then she could fix a time to bring her three children along to be inspected.

"Come along. Come along. Come along."

Madame led the way into a large airy studio. At the far end was a piano, at which a fair-haired girl sat thumping. Her name appeared to be Connie, for every time she paused in her thumping, a roar came from the end of the studio, "And again, Connie dear, and again."

The roar came from a large black-haired woman, dressed in a purple pleated skirt to the knees, her top half most indifferently held together by a purple jumper. She wore dirty pink cotton tights, and pink ballet shoes. Occasionally she worked at the exercises herself, and whenever this happened, her bosoms inside the purple jumper flopped and jumped about in so alarming a manner, that Rose really feared one would fly off.

All round the room, their small hands clutching a wooden bar, were hard-working little girls. Each child stood, for an incredible time, Rose thought, on the point of one toe, and with the other foot beat the ankle bone of the wretched foot so perilously balanced. After beating one ankle about fifty times, they changed feet and beat the other.

Occasionally a child paused, as though it would like to rest, but it was galvanised once more by the roar from the black-haired instructress. "And again, Connie dear, and again."

When at last the children were allowed to stop, they raced to the other end of the room, seized towels, and vigorously dried their necks, which appeared to be wringing wet after their efforts.

"No more bar," shouted the roaring one. "Character work."

This seemed to be the signal for every child to throw down its grubby towel, and fly out of the room, only to reappear one minute later in different shoes. Little flat patent leather shoes with ankle straps.

What followed left Rose speechless with amazement. All the children seemed to be made of indiarubber. The way they somersaulted, and cartwheeled, and threw each other about, and landed on the floor with their legs in so awkward and stretched a position, she thought they must split in half.

She turned to Madame.

"It's all very nice, wonderful in fact. But my children are quite ordinary little people. None of them could ever, ever do any of the things these children do."

"We shall see. We shall see. We shall see. Tuesday four o'clock, four o'clock, four o'clock." Madame added to Violet.

This was apparently dismissal, for with these words she walked into her office and shut the door.

CHAPTER 5

"I do think," Rose said to herself, "that before deciding about this dancing, I should ask 'Young Mr. Bray.' "

She rang up his office. He spoke to her himself, he still sounded kind. Rose had been afraid he might have slipped back into his graveside manner. Yes, he would see her the next morning.

Though naturally not quite the life they would choose, on the whole "Young Mr Bray" thought the dancing a good idea. Obviously the sooner the children could earn the better.

"You do know," he said tentatively, "that your income dies with you. You can do what you like about the house, but you've no money to leave."

"Oh! I do hope I live till they're all grown-up. If I should die I can't think what would happen." Rose shivered at the vision of penniless and stranded babies.

"Young Mr Bray" said he had been thinking of that too. He suggested a scheme to her. He should be appointed guardian together with Nannie. Rose should make a will leaving the house jointly between the three children. In the event of her dying during their childhood, the house could be sold to educate them.

Wills, Rose learnt, were not difficult things to make. He promised to have hers ready for signature next week.

The following Tuesday, Rose, Violet, Nannie, and the three children went to the Dancing Academy. They started badly. It was a hot day in May. Rose had decided that jerseys and knickers were as near as they could get to the correct dancing costume, a cotton romper, which she had seen worn by the pupils at the academy. Maimie and Tania had a scene about this in the nursery before they started. They would be too hot in jerseys. If they'd got to wear them they'd rather not go. They'd got new cotton frocks waiting in a drawer, why couldn't they wear them?

If Rose had heard the argument, she would probably have given in. But Nannie was a strict disciplinarian.

"I 'as me orders an' I sticks by 'em."

Three times Maimie put on her jersey backside foremost.

" 'Tisn't my fault, Nannie," she said crossly, "this jersey hasn't got no front."

Tania sat on the floor refusing to dress.

"Fank you, Nannie," she said as Nannie handed her her skirt. "On the whole I wasn't goin' this afternoon, it's too hot."

Finally when they did reach the hall, it was to find both Rose and Violet upset because they were late.

Daisy alone was supremely cheerful. She jigged up and down in her perambulator, her red curls bobbing.

"Me goin' to dance. Me goin' to dance."

"Little Balham show-off," muttered Maimie to Tania.

Tania said nothing. Her lips compressed with bad

temper, she shuffled down the road.

"Oh, lift your feet up, do," Nannie exclaimed exasperated.

"I won't lift up nothing, never, never, never," Tania whispered to herself.

They arrived panting at the top of the academy stairs, and were at once hurried into the dressing-room. On rows of wooden pegs hung grimy rompers. On the floor were piles of out-worn ballet shoes. Old cymbals and castanets lay about the room. The dust looked an inch deep.

Nannie exclaimed loudly :

"Give me your things to 'old, dears, there's nowhere fit to put anything down 'ere."

In the studio Madame was waiting. Her shrewd old blue eyes took in Maimie's beauty, and Daisy's red curls.

"What can they do? What can they do? What can they do?"

The children started to laugh, so Violet said hurriedly:

"Very little. Just try them with a few steps to see if they show promise. Then I should like a chat with you about them afterwards."

The children danced. Maimie graceful, but still bad-tempered, went sulkily through the few steps she had been taught.

Daisy joyfully hopped her way through some simple exercises.

Tania, her whole body rigid with dislike of the room and the whole situation, copied fairly accurately the movements she was shown by Madame.

"That'll do. That'll do. That'll do" Madame beckoned Violet into the office, and shut the door.

What was said there Rose never knew. But the result was that Madame offered to teach all three children for an incredibly low sum.

"I must talk it over with Nannie," Rose appealed to Violet.

It seemed to her a desperate step, tying the children up like that. The contracts covered such a number of years. Talk of licences, and the London County Council, frightened her.

She found Nannie waiting in the dressing-room with the children. She drew her to one side.

"She will take them, and it won't cost much. But oh, Nannie, I do hate it."

Nannie told Cook afterwards she hoped that God would overlook the lies she had told.

"For there was Miss 'oward lookin' that tired an' worried ——"

"She 'as bin lookin' thin lately," Cook interrupted ——"

—"an' 'er sayin' to me," Nannie went on, " 'I do 'ate it.' An' what was I to say? Acourse she 'ated it. Weren't no place for our children. But why should she 'ave them all on 'er 'ands till they're seventeen most like? No! 'Twasn't fair. So I says to 'er: 'Now, Miss 'oward, don't you be so silly. It may be a bit dirty,' I says. 'It mayn't be what we're used to,' I says. 'But theatricals is a trashy lot. If that Modom thinks as 'ow the children 'as talent 'tain't right to 'old 'em back.'

An' that done it! For on those very words, she turns round, goes back into Modom's office, and shuts the door."

Rose signed a contract, for all three children, that afternoon. She never knew that Violet gave endless free lessons in the Academy, to balance the low fees.

Maimie and Tania became very hard-working. The morning at school. Home to middle-day dinner. In the afternoon, if fine, a walk in the Park. Or if wet a visit to the Victoria and Albert. Home to tea. Then at five o'clock the Academy.

It did not come so hard on Maimie. She enjoyed the Academy. The other children admired her prettiness. She liked wearing a checked cotton romper, white socks, and pink ballet shoes. The exercises were rather a bore, doing the same thing so many times. But the dancing, the lively music, she found fun. At no time in her life could Maimie resist gaiety.

Tania hated the classes. She did not find the work hard. She was quick and very supple. But the place oppressed her. She loathed the other children. She disliked the dust. The musty smell in the cloakroom. Sometimes in the middle of a dance she would forget for a minute where she was, her legs would fly over her head, her spirits leap up. For one second she really danced. Then a greasy curl of another child touched her arm. Or her eye caught the pile of grimy towels lying on a bench in the corner. She grew stiff. All gaiety left her body. The real dancer of a moment before became an awkward little girl.

Daisy learnt in the mornings. She was the show

baby of the class. Very quick, very excited, very eager. Such simple steps as she was taught she picked up easily. She looked delicious bobbing about, a pleased smile on her round baby face, her red curls shining.

Tania, in her baby way, felt rather at odds with life. She liked her school in a placid kind of way. She rather liked walking in the Park, only Nannie went so slowly they never got anywhere. There must be such lots more to see. By the time they had walked up the Cromwell Road, turned into Greville Place, passed Emperor's Gate, and reached the Broad Walk, it was time to turn round and go home. The same with the Victoria and Albert. Always looking at those old dolls' houses, when there must be lots more interesting things.

"Let's go on," she would say tugging at Nannie's arm.

"You've seen all that's good for you," Nannie would reply. The truth being that she was convinced she would get lost if once she started wandering in that vast place.

Rose knew very little about children, and Nannie had a firm conviction that rightly brought up children went out in the afternoons. So nobody suggested that legs of people of five and seven, those same legs that were expected later to do two hours of the most violent exercise, might perhaps be the better for a rest.

Maimie, on returning from the Academy, would get half an hour in the nursery, or with Violet, before going to bed. But Tania was popped into her bath as soon as she got home, and after a glass of milk and two biscuits, expected to go happily to sleep. Her face grew rather sad-looking. She wasn't conscious of disliking things as they were, only nothing nice ever happened.

Then one Sunday in June, just before her sixth birthday, she found somebody. It was Mr. Williams, the ground-floor paying-guest. She was coming down the stairs, and she saw him in the hall on his hands and knees. He had an old motor bicycle. He had taken it to pieces and was reassembling it again. Tania hung spellbound over the stairs, and watched. She watched him for ten minutes, and he would never have known she was there, had he not mislaid a nut.

"Blast the damned thing," he muttered.

She slipped down the stairs, delicately picked up the missing nut, and laid it on his hand.

"God bless my soul, Tania! Are you a fairy? How did you know I wanted that?"

"I've been watching you," she explained.

But he was still puzzled.

"How did you know it was that nut I wanted?"

"I know'd what you was doing."

This was the beginning of a great friendship, born of mutual tastes. John Williams adored machinery. It was his job, when he had one. It was also his hobby. Tania loved machinery, too. To screw things together, to find out why something wouldn't go was an absorbing game. All the week she was too busy to play at anything, so on Sunday morning he always had something waiting for her. A clock that wouldn't go. A toy engine in need of repairs. A sewing-machine

50

that had stuck. They said very little to each other, but worked in that curious silent fellowship of the workman and his mate. But he gleaned fragments of her outlook on life.

Once she said:

"I do wish it was always Sunday."

"Why? Which is it you don't like, the school or the dancing classes?"

"The dancing."

"Pity you aren't a boy, you could have got a job in this line."

"If I was a boy I'd learn to fly."

"Why?"

"They goes so fast."

At Christmas the Academy woke up to violent activity. All three children became very unimportant. Their classes were cancelled. There was no room for them to work. Only people old enough to appear in pantomime mattered. Maimie was jealous of the older girls, it sounded to her a lovely life. Tania was thankful she was so young. The thought of appearing on the stage terrified her.

"Six more Christmases before I'll be old enough," she thought joyfully.

CHAPTER 6

The next few years were remarkably uneventful. A solid round of lessons and dancing for the children. A solid round of housework and ordering meals for Rose. But 1923 was a gala year. It started with measles.

All the children caught it. Daisy very badly. Nannie had an exhausting time. Maimie was cross, and bored, missing her friends. Daisy was so ill she could hardly be left for a moment. Tania was the only one who was happy. She frankly enjoyed the disease. To her it was a heavenly, and most unexpected holiday. As soon as she was well enough John Williams appeared with books on cars and aeroplanes. They discussed makes of engines, and horse-power. They decided what cars they would buy, and how fast they would go.

Maimie would listen to all this, hideously bored and, after John Williams had gone, grumble at Tania.

"My goodness! what can you see in those horrid dirty old cars. Pity you aren't Daisy, 'The Child Marvel,' then perhaps you'd earn enough to buy one, and could drive me about."

This glorious thought would start the children off on their pet game. It was a good game for busy people, because it could be played anywhere, and in odd moments. They called it "Families." Maimie as the eldest had first pick. She said how big her family was, and whether boys or girls. Tania had to have two less of each sex, and Daisy two less again. So when Maimie was bad-tempered, and wanted to be annoying, she would say:

"I'm playing 'Families,' and neither of you can play, 'cos I'm only having two children."

Maimie as the eldest had divine rights throughout the game. This often led to quarrels. For if she decided her children drove in a car, Tania's children weren't allowed one. When the game first started Tania checkmated this by travelling her children in an aeroplane. But Maimie soon put a stop to that by saying firmly:

"My children will travel by car and aeroplane."

"'Tisn't fair," Tania would protest. "Mine will have to go by horse, and you do know how I hate going slow."

Daisy liked her family to ride on donkeys. Nannie had ridden one on some glorious occasion, and often told them about it.

"Donkeys! She would!" The other two scoffed, and went on scornfully with the game.

On recovering from the measles, the children returned to work. Perhaps they were run down. For they promptly caught whooping-cough.

The Cromwell Road is a most unsuitable spot to have whooping-cough. Nannie would try and hurry them into the Park, but they all managed to whoop before they got there, and were looked at with fury by passing Nannies with small children and perambulators. Although the first one to catch the disease began whooping early in May, August found them still at it.

53

Both the schools were shut. London stuffy, and dusty. The children looking like shadows.

"We'll go away," said Rose.

Afterwards the children always marked time by that summer.

"It was before Sussex," they would say. Or, "it was after Sussex."

They stayed at Friston, a village on the downs above Eastbourne. But Rose had said they were going to Sussex. From that moment the word 'Sussex' represented their holiday, and epitomised everything that was nicest in life.

"Such 'Sussexly' chocolates. I do think my new frock's Sussex."

They went to Friston, because friends of Violet's lent them a cottage there. It was nobody's real choice. Nannie fancied Margate, she'd always heard the air was wonderful, and she had spent a day there once as a small child, and had never forgotten its glories. Rose, too, wished for the sea, as she believed it would be the quickest way to get rid of the children's coughs. But she would have chosen Folkestone or Bournemouth, where she had been herself taken to recover from childish ailments. The children had never been away before, so as long as they went somewhere, they didn't mind where it was.

They arrived at Friston about five o'clock on a gloriously sunny afternoon. Their cottage was away from the village, and looked out over the downs.

Maimie gazed out of the window. She was silent with amazement. Such a lot of space. She slipped a hand into Rose's:

"I suppose it's safe, but I wish there were more people about."

Tania ran outside. She stared at the grey rolling distance, with its stripings of coloured fields. At the low clouds hurrying by, making racing black shadows as they passed. She felt the wind blow against her body, it gave her a feeling of speed. She felt so uplifted, so terribly glad to be alive, that it hurt her physically, she had to lay her hand over her heart. Rose had followed her out.

"Do you like it, Tania?"

The child struggled for words. At last:

"It's nice," she said.

Daisy raced out on to the down-side.

"Oh Howdy," she called out, "what a stage!" and rapidly turned one cartwheel after another.

They had the sea breezes that Rose wanted, for every day, taking their lunch and tea with them, they went to Birling Gap.

On the beach they got to know a family of boys, who taught them to swim and the glories of catching prawns. The children had never known boys before. The boys had no sisters, and considered all girls delicate creatures, but even so they expected a far higher standard of physical courage from the children than had ever been expected of them before. With the result that before they left, they could all swim a little without one foot on the ground, and would fall about on the sharp slippery rocks while prawn-catching, covering their legs with scratches without a murmur.

On their first day's prawning, the youngest boy, who was not much older than Daisy, scraped his leg on a barnacle, and positively streamed with blood. The girls exclaimed in horror, and remarked on his bravery in not complaining.

"Goodness!" the eldest boy Geoffrey had replied, "I should just think he wouldn't. I'd like to hear him holloa at a little thing like that!"

The girls said nothing. Their standard up to date had been of the "kiss-it-and-make-it-well" variety. Not to complain when hurt? It was a new idea, but they quickly absorbed it. For that the boys should think well of them was the secret ambition of all three.

Rose and the boy's mother sat together on the beach. They took to each other, and would sit happily sewing and chatting for hours together, until an outburst of cat-calls from the rocks would warn them that their respective families were returning, anxious to be fed.

Nannie seldom came down to the beach. Sea breezes were all very well in their way, she said, but she didn't hold with all that unnecessary trapesing and scrambling about, when there was all that good air to be breathed by just sitting outside the cottage. The truth being that she was getting rather fat for strenuous exercise.

Sometimes, when the tide was wrong for prawns, there was cricket on the downs. The girls did not shine at this. Their life of lessons and dancing classes had left no room for games. But they made up in willingness and enthusiasm what they lacked in skill.

Truth to tell, the boys would have been disgusted if the girls had been any good.

"Cricket's not a woman's game."

Cricket showed the girls another point of view surprisingly different from their own. Maimie, disgusted with her bad batting, and to show that at any rate she was good at something, turned two rapid cartwheels and did a splits. But the boys, far from admiring, were shocked.

"I say! I wouldn't do that here," one of them said. "There are people about, they'll think you are showing off."

As all the children believed "showing off" to be their duty, this point of view amazed them. They said nothing to each other, but the words sank in. Dancing in front of people when they hadn't asked you to, that was "showing off," and showing off like that was a thing the boys despised. How very curious! But no more acrobatics appeared while they were in Sussex.

Tania was the favourite, because of her amazing knowledge of cars. She was as quick, or quicker than the boys, to spot a make of car as it flew by. She knew such a lot about their engines. What car she would like, and why. Geoffrey would talk to her by the hour, while they scrambled about. "She is a nice kid," he often told his mother.

On the last night before they left there was a supper picnic on the downs outside the cottage. The moon came up before they had finished. It was a lovely night. Tania discovered that she was not the only tongue-tied person in the world. She and Geoffrey were looking over the downs, which were a shining sheet of silver-grey. The sky was a mass of stars. The air had that odd, newly-washed smell of the downlands.

"Are you sorry you are going back to school to-morrow?" Tania asked.

He looked across the downs. And Tania looking up at him knew that he felt just as she did—sort of afraid that things could never be quite so lovely again—not exactly afraid of growing up—but that, too, somehow.

She said, "Looks nice, doesn't it?"

"Oh, not bad," he turned away embarrassed.

The families parted with promises of soon meeting again, of other jolly holidays, and seeing each other next time the boys were in London. Perhaps the boys forgot them, the girls never knew. They wrote for a bit, childish scrawling letters. Tania wrote regularly to Geoffrey, and just at first he wrote back, then he didn't answer, and didn't answer, so she stopped writing. They never met the boys again.

They returned to London the next morning. The Cromwell Road seemed incredibly stuffy, drab, and unbearable. They had carried away with them a last glorious glimpse of Sussex. It was a perfect morning, but there had been rain in the night, the downs looked so clean, the air smelt lovely. Walking down to where the bus stopped they picked handfuls of little mauve scabious. When they got to London Tania was still holding hers. She carried them up to the nursery and arranged them in a mug. She tried, as she looked at them, to bring back the downs. It seemed incredible that she had picked them only that morning. That the downs were still there without her. The sea still pouring over the rocks. And neither she nor Geoffrey there to see.

CHAPTER 7

The next day they started work. It was a very busy autumn. Madame had promised a programme from her children at a dancing matinée. Royalty would be present; rather minor Royalty, but still Royalty. A very grand affair. Daisy, to the disgust of her sisters, was to star. A solo dance. Première Danseuse of the Babies' Ballet.

"She will be insufferable after this," said Maimie. "Little Balham show-off!"

"She will," Tania agreed, "And the awfullest part you don't know, because you aren't in our class. On the programme she's to be called 'Babsy!' 'Babsy Whichart!' Such a disgrace to bring on our name!"

Maimie was really shocked. The minor aggravation of Daisy's stardom faded into the background.

"Oh, it mustn't be. We've always kept our name in honour. If she is going to call herself 'Babsy,' she mustn't use the 'Whichart.' "

"There's another thing," Tania sighed. "We've got to do a 'Pas de Trois' as the 'Whichart Sisters.' Imagine what fools we'll look!"

Maimie, however, privately considered this last good news. She was only expecting to appear as one of the "Corps de Ballet." That she was to be picked out in any way was pleasant hearing. So she reverted at once to what she called "The Daisy Scandal." "Don't let's stand for it. 'Howdy' must see Madame."

Rose was most unwilling. She hated seeing Madame, of whom she was secretly terrified. She could not see that it mattered terribly whether Daisy was called "Daisy" or "Babsy." Especially as Daisy herself had not minded, until she found her sisters were shocked and angry, and cold-shouldered her as though she had committed a crime. But in the end she did go because the children's family pride touched her.

"Poor darlings," she thought, "so delicious of them to be so proud, and after all it is their name, they invented it."

Madame was glad to see Rose. She considered her rather an ornament to her establishment. So very lady-like. So different from the mothers of most of the children. She agreed at once on Rose nervously explaining her errand:

"Of course, of course, of course."

She seized a pen overflowing with red ink, and with one dash erased the "Babsy" for ever.

But when the posters for the matinée appeared, Daisy found herself in worse disgrace. "A Special Matinée," it said. "By the Pupils of the Madame Elise Academy of Dancing. When the following children will appear." Here followed a list of star pupils, finishing up with—"And Little Daisy Whichart, The Wonderful Baby Dancer."

The children saw the poster on their way back from school. They stood solemnly in front of it, and read it in silence. Nannie, bursting with pride, read it too.

"Well!" said Maimie to Tania, "I think we'd better

61

be getting on. There's some people too common for us to know." She threw a withering look at Daisy, who began to cry.

"Oh, Maimie, I didn't know, truthfully I didn't know."

"To think," Tania said, "that this shameful thing is stuck up where all the school can read it. Why even the mistresses might see it."

"If they do," Maimie burst in, "I wouldn't wonder if we was all expelled, such shame for any school."

"Don't you listen to them, my blessed lamb," Nannie protested. "It's jealousy, that's what it is! Ordinary troupe children they are, while there's you dancing, all of your own, before Royalty."

"I'd rather be a troupe child for the rest of my life than be 'The Wonderful Baby Dancer.' Ugh!" exclaimed Tania ferociously, and she stalked on.

Maimie followed her.

"You stay with Nannie, 'Baby Daisy' " she called over her shoulder.

If Maimie and Tania were disgusted, the kitchen was bursting with pride. So were most of the boarders. Cook got hold of a poster, hung it in the kitchen, and showed it to all the tradesmen. Mrs. Williams came down to admire. So did the two women on the second floor. Violet almost swaggered.

"I spotted the kiddy's talent when she was three."

The other two could have borne all this fuss at home, if only the school had backed them up. But the school was far from angry, it was proud. They hung a poster on the gate. The matinée was for a laudable object. Royalty was patronising it. Daisy, who had been considered the least interesting of the sisters, sprang to a sudden fame.

Nobody except Rose understood exactly how the other two felt. Nannie openly said they were jealous.

"It isn't only that, Nannie," Rose tried to explain. "Of course they are a little jealous, it's only natural. But it's partly they hate having a show made of their name. I've so often laughed with them at all this wonder child stuff, and tried to show them that it's theatrical, and unnecessary, so they hate seeing Daisy making an oddity of herself. If she wasn't using the 'Whichart' they wouldn't have minded half as much".

The matinée was an enormous success. Daisy had a small triumph. She was very small for her age. With a pretty though rather commonplace little face, and a really lovely mop of red curls. She had very real gifts as a dancer. The "Pas de Trois" went well, it was a lively affair, and the fact that it was danced by three sisters appealed to the audience.

Nannie was so proud of her nurslings, and particularly of her godchild, that she couldn't enjoy herself in case something went wrong to mar the glory of the afternoon. She said to Cook who was sitting with her:

"I'm that fussed when those blessed lambs is on the stage, in case they does it wrong, or their knickers fall off or something."

Cook sniffed at this, and said if that was all, Nannie could sit back and take it easy, for from the look of them, there wasn't much in the way of knickers to fall anywhere.

Rose and Violet sat together. Curiously enough Rose had scarcely ever seen the children dance. Now she saw at once that Daisy had a chance of really reaching the top, if only she stuck at it and worked hard. And that Maimie and Tania had been well-trained. They struck her as being extremely proficient. She had always thought stage children rather pathetic, and she thought so again now, as she realised the years of hard work that lay behind those neat legs raised so easily over their heads. Those nimble cartwheels and splits, those pretty little professional gestures and hand-kissings, those bright smiles. It was Tania's steady bright smile that touched her the most. She knew the child hated her work, and yet she smiled. When the performance was over and she went behind, it was not for the brilliant Daisy that she first looked for, but for Tania.

"Darling, you were very good. I was very proud of all my children. But you do know, don't you, that as soon as you are old enough you can be trained for something else if you'd rather."

Tania didn't understand.

"Goodness! I must have been bad," she thought.

That Christmas Maimie had her first engagement. It was in a pantomime. She was one of a troupe of forty children; "Madame Elise's Wonder Mites."

The immediate result of Maimie's becoming a wage-earner was that she suddenly became very childish. From being very much the eldest in the family, she almost degenerated into baby talk. In the theatre she was treated as if she was about six. She was the youngest of the troupe, many of whom, in spite of socks and baby ways, were seventeen. She found she was expected to behave childishly. The grown-ups in the cast, if they spoke to her at all, petted her, pulled her curls, and asked her if she liked dolls; she who hadn't touched a doll for years. The result was rather unbearable at home. She lisped, she wanted her hand held when she crossed a road. Tania was only voicing the opinion of the entire household, when she said in a burst of fury:

"Would you like a puff-puff on a little string to pull to the theatre?"

It wasn't altogether Maimie's fault. Being the eldest had deprived her of much baby petting. She adored it now she had it. And no star of a musical comedy ever played to her gallery better.

The pantomime ran well into April. Rose banked the whole of the child's earnings each week. They weren't large, but they accumulated to a nice sum. Violet wanted her to spend some of it on Maimie's clothes, but she refused:

"It's worth everything to me to know the children have something saved. It makes me shiver to think of what might happen to them if I should die."

With the end of the pantomime Maimie grew up again. She was tired of behaving like a baby. Besides, it was difficult to be babyish, and yet extract the respect from the others due to the wage-earner. Her family were delighted; better, they thought, a rather cocky Maimie, than a posey Maimie. Their delight was short-

65

lived, for two months later she 'got religion,' and got it badly. It seemed to attack her suddenly, but was really the result of a schoolgirl crush for her form-mistress, who was very high-church. It upset the household, particularly on Sundays, for she insisted on attending High-Anglican Mass. Nannie had always taken the children to a Children's Service on Sunday afternoons. She had been brought up Chapel, but she took the children to Church, as she said it was her duty; all gentry being Church. But take Maimie to High-Anglican Mass she would not.

"Next thing we knows, Miss 'oward, she'll 'ave gone over to Rome, an' then where'll she be?"

Rose, who had stayed at home on Sundays, considering it a well-earned day of rest, decided she must take the child herself. Maimie's nature had always worried her slightly. "Perhaps religion will be a help to her," she thought. She found she rather enjoyed the service. She was tired, and in spite of Maimie's shocked lifted eyebrows, she sat most of the time and gave herself up to enjoying the music. She had been brought up Low Church, so she couldn't follow the ritual; "All that fussy business up at the altar," as she described it to herself, and she did not believe that in spite of all Maimie's deep bowings, and crossings, and unexpected kneelings, that she did either.

Maimie said she must be confirmed. Rose, determined to do the right thing, asked the advice of the High-Church form-mistress, Miss Marmaduke, who said:

"Oh, she must go to Father Sutch, a marvellous man; just the influence Maimie needs in her life."

Rose doubted this, and took a great dislike to Miss Marmaduke, whose feelings became so much for her when she spoke of Father Sutch, that she almost slobbered. Still, if Miss Marmaduke recommended Father Sutch, Maimie would insist on being prepared by him. So to Father Sutch Rose went.

She found him a tall, good-looking man, dressed in a cassock and biretta. Although very busy, he was very kind, and showed her round his church, and asked her to admire his new lamp hanging before the Reserved Sacrament. He fixed the hours for Maimie's classes, and then left her in a hurry to hear some confessions. She felt completely confused, and tried, by reading the notice board outside, to discover whether the church was really Church of England or not. "Oh well," she thought, "I suppose one religion will suit Maimie as well as another." She climbed wearily on to a bus and went home.

Maimie's confirmation was the cause of a real quarrel between her and Tania. The two girls now shared the old day-nursery, while Daisy and Nannie slept in the night-nursery. Rose had turned a small empty boxroom into a sitting-room for the children, and they fed with everyone else in the dining-room on the ground floor. This arrangement had worked beautifully, for Maimie and Tania were the greatest friends, and shared their room with complete amicability. But the weight of Father Sutch's teachings changed Maimie. First she went in for such deep meditations, and said such long prayers, with such bowings and crossings, that Tania, who considered it "showing off," was driven nearly mad. "Showing off" in the Dancing Academy sense might be right; "showing off" at your prayers most certainly was not. Then one day she came into their bedroom to find in the corner a small altar. They possessed a little table; on this Maimie had put an old red tablecloth, two small candlesticks with red candles, a vase of red flowers, and in the centre a cheap wooden cross. To Maimie it was beautiful. She might be carried away by her emotions, and a love of outward show, but she was honestly straining after something. She wanted to be good, she wanted to please Miss Marmaduke, and Father Sutch, and incidentally, God. She couldn't help it that subconsciously she pictured people saying: "That's a wonderful child, dancing all day, and then coming home to her little altar at night." She hoped people would feel goodness emanating from her: "She's a real example, that child."

She had been to her confirmation class. She felt quite uplifted. She ran into her bedroom to spend a few minutes kneeling at her altar, in the way Father Sutch had taught her. She found her flowers, and cross, and candles lying on the floor, and Tania with the tablecloth clutched in her hands, her face white with rage.

"How dare you turn our bedroom into a church; how dare you!"

Maimie screamed, she completely lost control. She seized Tania by her hair, kicked her, and might have knocked her senseless, had not Rose and Nannie rushed in.

Rose was in a quandary. Tania had been very naughty. A cross was a sacred symbol, it was terribly wrong to throw it on the floor. Wrong in any case to throw Maimie's things about. Yet if you hated show and fuss, how annoying to find an altar in your bedroom. What a climax of aggravation after having borne with Maimie for weeks, in a state of perpetual prayings.

That night she took Tania to sleep with her. At first she scolded; Tania looked like a mule. Then she said:

"Tania, dear, if you can't or won't see it was wrong, surely you can see it was silly. If you had come to me I could have reasoned with Maimie, found her somewhere else to put it, made her take it all down. Now you've made that impossible. It's you who should be punished. It was wrong of Maimie to hit you, but what you did was far worse."

"Oh, Howdy, she's so aggravating."

"I'll tell you a secret, Tania; it aggravates me, too. I hate slops and all this religious fervour strikes me that way. But we aren't all made alike, perhaps it's a help to Maimie. You don't suppose that I've always liked going to these services with her, they are not a bit the sort of services I like and understand. But I don't refuse to take her. Instead, I try and see the funny side of it all. I'm ashamed to say I find a lot in that service she goes to that I think very funny, really the oddest things they do. I don't, of course, suggest you should

69

laugh at Maimie's prayers, but I've found you can bear almost anything if you can see its funny side."

The next morning Tania apologised to Maimie, and helped her to rearrange the altar. This she did with the utmost seriousness, but occasionally the corners of her mouth twitched.

The following Sunday, Maimie, coming home from church, found Tania in their bedroom with Daisy. Tania had a tambourine, Daisy a drum. They were singing in shrill and exaggeratedly nasal voices, "Nearer my God to Thee."

"What the Devil?" asked Maimie.

"Ssh," whispered Tania, "please don't interrupt. Me and Daisy have joined the Salvation Army. You'll often hear us having a private service together, I expect. You don't mind, do you?"

Maimie bore with the hymn-singing, and the tambourine and drum, for three days. Then she removed her altar.

Rose, who learnt from Nannie what had happened, wondered if she ought to interfere. But instead, she squared it with her conscience by giving Maimie an exceptionally nice white frock for her confirmation.

Maimie's religious phase held all through that year, and right through the run of another pantomime, until it would have surprised none of her family if she had become a nun. For during all those months she regularly and rapturously attended her church, made her confessions to Father Sutch, and embarrassed and upset the household by fasting on every conceivable occasion. The fast days were the cause of endless strife. She never knew it was going to be a fast until the very day itself; when she would learn about it from Miss Marmaduke, who, pale and difficult, after an early and fasting rise for Mass, followed by a frugal and hurried breakfast, vented her exhaustion on her class. Maimie, on reaching home, would say with a resigned air:

"Did I remember to tell you I wouldn't be taking any meat to-day?"

Nannie, who was a firm believer in a good solid meat middle-day dinner, was exasperated. And Cook, hurriedly preparing eggs, would mutter:

"Religion is as religion does. Givin' extra work ain't my idea of religion."

But early in the new year all this changed. Her faithful keeping of fasts abated; she no longer insisted on such rigorous church-going; she allowed Tania's preparation for confirmation by a handy, though Low Church parson round the corner, to pass without a murmur. She seemed her normal self; the whole household sighed with relief, and wondered why. The truth being she'd fallen in love.

It happened at the end of the run of the pantomime. Dancing off the stage one night, with the rest of the troupe, she caught her foot, and slightly sprained her ankle. It wasn't bad, but she made the most of it. There came to her aid, to carry her upstairs, the young man who played The Count. The Count not being an important rôle in a pantomime, Maimie had hardly noticed the young man before. But now his kindness, together with his large brown eyes, won her heart. His name was Eric Ericson. "What a beautiful name," thought Maimie, "and how suitable for so handsome an actor." Unaware that outside the theatre he was known as Sam Rosenblaum, and that he was a hard-working young man, doing a nice trade in cheap dresses and silk stockings, and that pantomime jobs were only a side line, found for him by his uncle, Moses Shultz, who was an agent dealing with such things. Maimie, not knowing all this, thought him not only a very handsome young man, but a great actor. Secretly, she boiled with indignation at the way "The Dame" and her comic son got all the laughs even when Eric was on the stage. The audience even went on laughing when Eric was speaking, such a shame! When a person had so few lines, they ought at least to be heard.

Eric was completely unaware of Maimie's admiration for him. To him she was just a nice little kid. "Damn pretty, too!" He considered her a baby, and would have been quite shocked if he had known that by two or three kind words, and a look from his large brown eyes, he had made her grow up. She ceased to be a petted child, and aped the manners of the grown-up chorus girls. She found chances to stand about in the wings, away from the other children and the matron, in the hope that he would come and speak to her. Sometimes he did. He would say:

"How are we to-night, Kiddy? Foot all right?" or, "Enjoying yourself, Kiddy?"

Desperately she would try and think of answers to these questions, bright interesting answers, that would hold him a minute. One night, greatly daring, she blurted out:

"Do you live far from here?"

"Down Russell Square way," he answered casually, and walked on to the stage.

The next morning at school Maimie, studying a map of London, learnt that the British Museum wasn't far from Russell Square. The pantomime was nearing its end, there were only three matinées a week now, that meant three free afternoons, for her dancing classes were suspended during the weeks she worked at night. So at dinner she said:

"This afternoon I should like to go to the British Museum."

Rose looked at her, horrified. Was high art to follow high religion? Were she and a weary Nannie to trail after Maimie to every museum and picture gallery in London?

Nannie merely asked comfortably:

"And for why, dear?"

"Well," Maimie explained, "it's the sort of place everyone ought to go to."

"An' so you shall some day," Nannie agreed, "but to-day there's me takin' Tania an' Daisy to the dancin', an' Miss 'oward 'as a 'eadache. But I tell you what, you're gettin' a big girl now, you can go by yourself to the Victoria an' Halbert."

Maimie set out, in her hand she clasped a shilling. Steadily she walked up the Cromwell Road, until she reached the turn for Gloucester Road Station. There she boldly took a ticket for Russell Square. She spent from half past two till four o'clock wandering round Russell Square, and the little roads behind it. Three times she passed the shop where her Eric was serving customers with cheap silk stockings. But she never looked in. At last, very bad-tempered, she went home to tea.

Before the pantomime finished, she screwed up her courage and asked Eric for a photograph. He promised he would bring one, but he kept forgetting. She was in a perfect fever of anxiety. Then on the last night he remembered:

"There's a present for a good little girl."

And he gave her not just a postcard, but a large shiny photograph, and on the corner he had written, "To little Maimie from Eric"; and underneath in smaller writing, "Count your blessings," one of his few lines from the pantomime.

Maimie persuaded Nannie to take her to Woolworths', and there she found a handsome imitation silver fame. She put Eric in it, stood him in the middle of the mantelpiece, and hung about self-consciously for Tania's exclamation of envy and admiration. Tania exclaimed all right, but all she said was:

"My God! what an Ike."

CHAPTER 8

The following Christmas, 1925, was Tania's first pantomime. She was one of a troupe of twelve speciality children dancers. She was not in the same pantomime as Maimie, and had no friends in the troupe. They were playing "Red Riding Hood" twice daily, in a theatre in South London. The whole thing was a misery to her. Ever since her twelfth birthday last June, she had known it must happen; she kept saying to herself, "Next Christmas I'll be for it." Yet when the pantomime auditions started she still hoped. Perhaps she'd be too plain. She got a stye on her eye; she was delighted; surely no manager would engage a child who had styes on its eyes. But when the manager of "Red Riding Hood," who was incidentally the manager of dozens of other pantomimes, engaged her troupe, he never looked at Tania. He just stood in the stalls, with a large cigar in the corner of his mouth, and a handsome Astrakhan collar on his coat, and while they danced gave an occasional groan. Sometimes he looked at their legs, more often he stared at the ceiling; Tania wondered which caused the groans. She was very hopeful that they wouldn't be engaged, he obviously wasn't enjoying himself. But when they had finished he said sadly to Madame:

"I suppose they'll do. Look a bit better when they're dressed up."

The whole business of playing in pantomime she

found a bore. She hated the depressing and smelly neighbourhood where they played. She hated travelling on the Underground with such an obvious troupe of child performers, with their skinny bare knees, and gum boots, and small attaché cases. She hated the interval between the matinée and the evening performances, when they had tea, and rested in their dressing-room smelling of grease-paint and hot clothes. She would bring down a book, and, following the adventures of speed-kings, would try to forget her surroundings. The Matron was very kind to her, found her a quiet corner in which to read, and scolded the other children if they bothered her. She would often talk to the child on their journeys to and fro, and took a real interest in her. It was a help, but it couldn't stop Tania loathing the pantomime.

She never complained about it to Rose, for Violet had told her they needed the money. But to Maimie at bed-time she unburdened her heart:

"I know you like it, Maimie, so it's all right for you. But I hate it, hate it, hate it! Oh! how I wish I was old enough to say I wasn't well, and get a day off sometimes."

In March the pantomime came to an end. Tania went back to her round of lessons and dancing classes. Then in the following autumn auditions began again.

That December Maimie reached the advanced age of fifteen. She ceased to be a juvenile; she was too tall. So Madame got her into a chorus. This changed her. The position of the chorus in a pantomime is so different from the position of the children. The children are so supervised and watched. The chorus utterly free. Maimie felt this change at the first rehearsal. It was unexpected. She had never realised it would be like that. She was just going into the chorus instead of joining the children, because she was so tall. Then she grasped that the doors had opened. She was free. Away from Matron. Earning her own living. A grown-up person.

When the pantomime finished she told Rose she was sick of school; if she could get another job she wouldn't go any more. Rose protested:

"You are only fifteen, darling. I'd like you to stay another two years at least. You needn't work. I am glad you can get pantomimes at Christmas because it means you've something saved, but as far as the school is concerned I can afford the fees."

"It's the money I want. And the sooner I put myself in the way of getting some, the better. You know, Howdy, it seems to me that having money is the only thing that really matters. If you've got money you can do what you like, go where you like. People always seem extra nice to the rich. If you're poor people are kind to you. Who the hell wants kindness!"

"Money can't buy happiness, you know," Rose said softly.

"Oh, my God! Fancy handing that slop out to me. If ever people ought to know that money is happiness, it's us. Look at us! Taking in boarders. Too few servants. Too few clothes. Us children dancing to help things out. Then look at some of the girls at school. Everything they want. Money poured on them. And they taking it as their right. Why not us? I swear to you, Howdy, I won't be poor. I don't care how I get money, but I'll get it somehow."

"I wish you wouldn't feel like that, Maimie; money is not so important as all that. I've enjoyed a lot of my life, and I've never had any."

"Oh you! You're one of 'The Saints of Earth,' who 'in concert sing.' Look at you! You could have had just enough to be bearable if you hadn't adopted us three."

"My dear, I'm very far from a saint. You and I look at life from quite a different angle."

"We do," agreed Maimie with fervour.

"But I hope you'll see things differently when you grow up."

"You watch me!"

In the end Maimie remained on at school, as she couldn't get another job. But to the dancing classes she would not go, saying she danced every bit as well as she had any need to, and goodness knows she'd been at it long enough. She made Rose miserable by insisting on drawing out all her savings from the bank. She was over the school-leaving age, she couldn't be prevented. But it seemed the most heartbreaking waste of the earnings of three pantomimes, to see it spent in a week on rubbishy showy clothes. But Maimie bitterly resented interference, she wanted a good time. And a good time was going out with boys. She adored 'boys.' Some of the ones she knew had cars; they all had enough money to take her to the pictures. In her new showy clothes she was a great success. Rose asked her to come in early, not to go out again after supper. But it only made her cross:

"Oh, don't fuss, Howdy. You put me on the stage when I was twelve, so it's too late to keep me in cotton wool."

"Let 'er be, Miss 'oward," Nannie advised. "If we tries to look after 'er too much, next job she 'as she'll be off on 'er own. She's the wild kind. A bit of 'er father and 'er mother, too, I should say."

That Christmas of Maimie's emancipation Tania worked hard in another pantomime. It was under the same management as "Red Riding Hood," but it was "Dick Whittington" this time. Except for the title, it was extraordinarily the same as the one before. She did the same dances, with the same children, wearing almost the same clothes, and singing songs which, though very new, had exactly the same themes. She hated it rather more than the year before, if that were possible. After the last performance she came home so glowing with happiness that Rose asked her what had happened. Tania answered with the last lines of the pantomime:

"And now we've had enough of this and that,
    Let's say farewell to Whittington and Cat."

The rest of the year was full of exceptionally hard work for the two younger girls. Tania was training as one of a speciality quartette of children acrobatic dancers that Madame hoped to place in a west-end pantomime. It was Daisy's last year of consistent training. By the next spring she would be old enough to start work. After that, although of course she would work and practise all the years she remained on the

79

stage, her actual lessons and training would be necessarily interrupted. Madame was enormously proud of her, and worked her very hard. The child, except for school and her daily walk, was seldom off her toes. Madame would watch her with tears in her eyes:

"Goo' gir', goo' gir', goo' gir," she would breathe ecstatically.

Tania slogging away with her quartette found all this admiration for "The child marvel" hard to bear. She didn't exactly grudge Daisy her success, but why had God picked on Daisy's legs as the ones to do even the most impossible exercises with no effort at all? If it was extra hard work that made Daisy so brilliant, she could have borne with it, but it wasn't; it was merely the result of the most blatant favouritism on the part of heaven.

"Oh my goodness! that child is the prize poodle of the academy," she sighed to Maimie.

"You wait till she really starts," Maimie said. "The Child Wonder! The little Star! There'll be no holding her back."

Tania's year of hard work was rewarded. After several nerve-racking auditions the quartette got their contract for a west-end pantomime.

"Thank goodness!" Tania said joyfully. "No trailing out into the tiger country this year. Twenty minutes from door to door. That's the job for this child!"

Maimie got into the chorus of the same show. It was "Aladdin," and a far more elaborate entertainment than any of their previous efforts. All the dances were to be produced by Dolly Kismet. His was a name notable in the theatre world, for he produced the dances for practically every musical comedy and revue in the West-End.

Dolly spotted Maimie at the first rehearsal.

"How old are you, Kiddy?"

"Sixteen."

"All right, Baby, we must keep an eye on you."

He put her in the centre of the front row. She didn't know it, but he watched her. Her work he placed at once. Very well trained, but no special ability, and less ambition. But the girl herself! What a looker! What a cute baby! Rather young of course— still he liked them young—looked innocent—but then you never knew—he hoped she was innocent—more fun that way—he loved teaching a babe.

The next day he kept her back after rehearsal, to show her a step, he said, that she hadn't got just right. He put his arm round her, and they danced it together. He let his hand slip casually further up her body. Yes, she was innocent all right, all right; didn't know a thing.

The following morning he called her back again, some other excuse. He told her she was a good girl, and lightly kissed her.

Maimie was amazed. He that was such a god, to kiss so unimportant a person as herself. Glowing, and treading on air, she left the theatre. From that morning she gave him a dog-like devotion. She gazed at him all day and dreamt of him all night.

Tania felt very differently about Dolly. Now that

81

she was over fourteen she was allowed to travel backwards and forwards on the Tube, with only Maimie as escort. On their journeys Maimie learnt that Tania didn't see Dolly as a god at all, to her he was a holy terror, who expected a girl's legs to do things they never could.

"Imagine! he complained of us to Madame, and she said it was difficult, but that anything a producer wanted her children could do! Oh! he is a prize cow that man. Oh, Maimie! how my legs do ache."

Dolly found Maimie eating her lunch on the stage. She and Tania were devouring sandwiches and fruit packed by Cook.

"Hullo!" he said.

Maimie smiled coyly, and said nothing. Tania, in her horror at meeting her enemy in her off-work hours, took too large a bite of sandwich and choked. Maimie beat her roughly and furiously on the back, disgusted at this gross behaviour before her god. Dolly only smiled:

"Take a drink of something, Kiddy."

"I'll get a glass of water," Tania wheezed, and fled.

Dolly sat down beside Maimie. He ran his fingers through her hair.

"You've got pretty hair, Baby."

Maimie only smiled.

"And a pretty face, and a very pretty little figure"; his hand wandered over her.

Her experience with the boys who had taken her motoring and to the pictures had left her quite unprepared for Dolly. She thought: "Surely it must

82

have been an accident, he couldn't have meant to touch me quite like that. Not there!"

Dolly's penchant for Maimie was not unnoticed by the rest of the chorus.

"It's a damned shame!"

"She's only a kid!"

"Somebody ought to say something!"

But nobody did, it was nobody's business. One of the girls did warn Maimie.

"You be careful of Dolly. He's an awful little rotter. Got no end of girls into a mess. Dirty little bastard!"

Maimie was flattered to think the other girls had noticed Dolly's interest in her. They were all so much older than she was, what fun if they were jealous. As it happened, as soon as the pantomime was produced, she saw far less of Dolly, and never saw him alone. He told her he was going to take her to a dance, and she was wild with excitement at the thought. Alone at a dance with Dolly, envied by everyone; even the principals were proud to be seen about with Dolly. As it happened the dance was never arranged. A rush of spring productions kept the extremely successful Dolly furiously busy. Maimie, not realising what had happened, supposed he had lost interest, and was depressed and dissatisfied with herself. With the result that she was unbearably cross and difficult at home. She quarrelled with Tania, which was not difficult. For Tania's nerves, at the end of a long run of twice-daily performances, were none too good. She even managed to quarrel with Daisy, which was quite a feat, as Daisy hated quarrelling. Rose was in despair; she wasn't feeling at all well, and this to her unaccountable bickering among the children, upset her terribly, as she'd no idea how to tackle it. Only Nannie remained unmoved:

"Well, what's a bit of temper? I'll try 'em with a Seidlitz."

But in the spring, when the pantomime finished, the air cleared. Dolly had not forgotten Maimie— "Poor little kid; must get her a bit of fun—teach her a bit of life—show her a thing or two."

His first step towards her education was to get her into the chorus of a musical comedy, for which he was producing the dances. The musical comedy was like a new world to Maimie. The chorus girls were so grand, not only in their clothes, but in their outlook on life. They were completely different from the chorus girls in the pantomime. In fact, Maimie discovered that to have been in a pantomime chorus was a thing to be ashamed of, and forgotten as soon as possible. Then the work! They worked as hard as she had done in the juvenile troupes. Came down on the stage every morning and worked like slaves. Chorus girls in a pantomime never did that. They worked fairly hard at rehearsals while the producer's eye was on them, but after the first night they slacked off. Of course in a pantomime there was all that work, marching up and down the grand staircase at the finale. There was none of that in a musical comedy. But Maimie almost regretted having stopped her dancing lessons. She was out of practice for the really hard and skilled work required of her.

Rose tried to persuade her to save. She might as well have talked to the wind. She earned three pounds a week, of which she paid twenty-five shillings towards the housekeeping; Violet and Nannie had seen to that. The rest went on clothes. Little rubbishy hats and frocks, in shocking taste, and little fragile crêpe-de-Chine underclothes, which, as Nannie said:

"Fell to pieces in your 'ands."

The girl was quite independent. Rose was afraid to criticise anything for fear that she would flaunt off in a temper and live on her own. Her morning rehearsals made school out of the question. Rose did ask if she would like to throw up the job, and go on with her lessons, but all she answered was:

"Would I hell!"

As soon as the musical comedy was really running, Dolly got her a place in a cabaret. This meant more work, but it also meant more money. She dressed better, not in better style, but she had more clothes. She got to know a lot of men. She went about everywhere; her face was always in the picture papers; she was quite a success. She enjoyed it all. The rush, the excitement, the popularity. But she still wasn't seeing much of Dolly.

That summer he took her education in hand. He took her on the river; he took her motoring in the country. Rose, who had caught sight of him, was terrified. She was afraid to say anything; Maimie would soon be seventeen, always a difficult age to handle, but doubly so when the girl is independent. She asked

Nannie's advice. Nannie was of the opinion that the situation was beyond earthly powers.

"We can only trust in God, Miss 'Oward," she said devoutly.

She repeated this to Cook, who said that if God was keeping His eye on Maimie, it was her opinion He wouldn't have much eye left for the rest of the world.

Dolly took Maimie to his flat. It had a long, low, black sitting-room, splashed here and there with gold cushions. It was decorated with photographs of Dolly. Maimie thought it beautiful. He pulled off her hat, and ruffled her hair. She looked out of the window at a long stretch of blue-grey London view. She heard a clock strike. Dolly from behind slipped his hands under her armpits. She shivered. He pulled her round to face him.

"Little innocent Baby."

Maimie moved away with a jerk.

"I think I'd better go home," she laughed nervously. "It does seem silly, but do you know, I feel frightened, Dolly."

He pulled her down beside him on the divan. His hands slowly stroked her. Soothed her. She felt almost sleepy. He put his lips to hers. She turned her body towards him.

When she put on her hat she couldn't look at him. She was amazed when she got into the street to find that she didn't look different. Nobody stared. Nobody seemed to guess.

It was in bed that night that she first got frightened. Suppose she had a baby! People did. She calculated; two and a half weeks before she would know. Heavens! Two and a half weeks; oh, if only she could tell someone. She slept badly. She got thin. And only one week gone. Another week and a half—how endure it? By the end of the second week, if she slept at all, it was to wake up with a violent jump, her hands wet with perspiration. Nannie, who had watched her with growing anxiety, decided that she must speak to the child. She knocked on her door.

"Come in," Maimie sang out joyously. Her eyes were shining, her cheeks pink with happiness, she had never looked better.

"I 'aven't thought you lookin' well, Maimie dear."

"Rubbish! Nannie, I've never felt better."

Back in her bedroom, Nannie sighed as she picked up her darning.

CHAPTER 9

The musical comedy finished, but the cabaret still went on. Then Dolly got Maimie into a revue. In this she had a real part. For as well as being in the chorus, she appeared as a maid, and said: "This way, sir". Up till then all her speaking on the stage had been done with the rest of the chorus. They had said brightly altogether, "Oh, do tell us," or "Here he is, girls, what fun!" Her solo line impressed her sisters in a way a solo dance would never have done.

"You can call yourself a real actress," Daisy said enviously.

Tania, who was also impressed, merely remarked: "Let us know when you are playing Lady Macbeth".

Dolly gave parties in his flat. To one of them Maimie took Tania as a treat. She was so very much accepted among Dolly's friends, so very much Queen of the flat, that she thought it a great pity some of her family couldn't be there to see. They'd never suspect anything, they'd only admire the way she was getting on in the world. So she took Tania as an audience.

It was not a success. Tania, who just had her fifteenth birthday, looked, and was, a long-legged schoolgirl. She sat awkwardly on the divan, her knees together, her feet splayed out. Refusing cocktails and cigarettes, she held grimly to her cup of tea and, in spite of everyone, made an exceedingly hearty meal. She scarcely spoke a word, but in the intervals of eating, she stared. She told Rose about it afterwards:

"Howdy, I was struck dumb. Imagine it! The flat's all black with gold cushions, rather like that transformation scene we had in 'Red Riding Hood.' And as if seeing that little hound of a man in the flesh wasn't awful enough, his photographs were all over the walls! There was just the loveliest view though, Howdy; far too good for him. Still, I don't suppose he ever sees it, the room looks as though it usually had the blinds down. He's not the sort to stand much light. Gracious! the people were queer; frightfully noisy, knowing each other most terribly well, and calling each other 'darling' every other word. They all looked frightfully rich, the most expensive clothes, diamond watches and things. I never found out who any of them were, but they must all have been stars, I think, because they talked of people like Gladys Cooper and Evelyn Laye by their Christian names, so they must have known them. They all kept saying the same things over and over again: 'Oh, my dear! have you heard how that bastard so-and-so treated so-and-so?' And when everybody had said no, they told a long story about how—somebody had pinched somebody else's laugh—and somebody else had their best song cut, because someone else was jealous—and somebody else had slammed their dressing-room door in somebody else's face. Oh! what a dreary afternoon."

"And Maimie?" Rose asked nervously. "Did she seem to be enjoying herself?"

Tania hesitated. Privately, she had been disgusted with Maimie. "The poor fish!" she thought. Fancy being anything as unpleasant as Dolly Kismet's bit, and get so little out of it. Why! she might have been his servant!—'Maimie, there's no more gin,' and Maimie went and got it—'Maimie, I'm cold, do shut the window,' and Maimie jumping up to do it. Still, one couldn't very well say all that to Howdy, who wouldn't understand being a bit, even if, as one strongly suspected, she had been Whichart's mistress." So she said casually:

"Oh, Maimie adores that kind of thing. She made herself useful showing everyone Dolly's newest of newest photographs. I was the world's frost because, when she showed them to me, I said: 'Are you getting commission on these?' Anyway, I wasn't a howling success, because whatever Maimie thinks of Dolly, I think him a loathly slug, and I expect I show it."

Rose sighed.

"He sounds terrible. Maimie's an awful anxiety to me, Tania."

Tania longed for the power of showing affection. Rose looked so yellow. So tired. It was ridiculous to worry over Maimie, whose future was as obvious as though it were written on the sky. How could a person like Howdy hope to change it? Couldn't she see? She laid her hand casually on Rose's arm. Then, ashamed of such a display, snatched it away as though it had been burned, and said hurriedly:

"Oh, well, everything will be all right, don't worry".

But Rose did worry. Maimie wasn't her only trouble. Nannie was her confidante:

"The boarders are all leaving. Mr. Williams has got a job at last, just what he wants; a nice engineering job in the north. I'm very pleased for them, but——Then the second floor are going, they think they'd rather live in the country. Most sensible of them, I told them so; their income will go much further. But that leaves only Miss Grimshaw. Of course there's Maimie's twenty-five shillings a week, but her revue won't last for ever. I feel terribly anxious. I feel as though I shall never find any more boarders, certainly none as nice as these."

Nannie made the clucking, soothing sounds she had made to the babies when they were very small:

"There, there, my lamb, it will all come right. You go and 'ave a good talk with that there Young Mr. Bray.' Maybe 'e'll suggest somethin'."

Rose saw 'Young Mr. Bray'. She told him all her worries. He listened in silence, then he said:

"Forgive me, but have you seen a doctor?"

"Me! No. Why?" She trembled. She had been feeling ill; not very ill, but a little ill, for a long time. Was it so obvious? What did he suspect?

"I should try Henry Carfax; clever fellow, good at diagnosis. I'll write down his name and address for you. He's not so expensive as some of them, but I'd trust his opinion before all the bigwigs gathered together."

"Does he specialise in any disease?"

'Young Mr. Bray' hesitated for the fraction of a second. Then he said cheerfully:

"Yes, on nerves; tired nerves. I expect he'll send

you away for a couple of months, and leave those troublesome wards of yours to Nannie for a bit."

"Oh nerves! Is that what I look like? Well, if that's all, I needn't worry. Away for a couple of months indeed! When I'm managing so badly as it is."

"Whatever Carfax orders, I want you to come and tell me. There may be ways I could help. Promise?" 'Young Mr. Bray' looked serious. Then he went on more lightly, "Now for your real worries———"

He thought the time had come to sell the house. It might go as a small hotel, or boarding house, or perhaps someone would convert it into flats. He suggested putting it in the market at once. Right away Rose could start looking for an inexpensive flat. Cheap to run. No need to take in boarders. Altogether more sensible. All the children old enough to work now. They wouldn't earn much, but enough to help. Rose must not worry. There was no cause.

Sitting on her bus going home, Rose tried to picture her house as an hotel, or flats, run entirely as a business concern. She remembered herself and the Brigadier, getting out of a hansom cab—"This is the house, my darling. I hope you're going to like it."— The years that followed. Looking back, she seemed to have spent those years waiting—Waiting for him to arrive—Waiting to see what mood he was in when he did arrive—Waiting to know what he'd like her to wear. That November day when he went away; such greyness; such a numb, dreadful feeling when the door slammed. "Poor house," she thought, "all my life has happened in you, and now I'm going to sell you as an hotel, or flats. What ingratitude!" She had a crumpled bit of paper in her hand; on it was written:

Mr. H.B. Carfax, and an address in Queen Anne Street. She looked at the paper and shivered: "Oh well! Perhaps I'd have had to leave the house anyway."

Two important things happened on the same day. Rose saw the doctor. And Madame saw Rose.

Mr. Carfax was a kind man. He examined Rose. He asked a lot of questions. He said he thought there must be an operation. He wasn't sure. There were certain tests he would like to make. Rose looked at him:

"I'm not a coward, Mr. Carfax. Tell me what you suspect."

Arriving home, full of courage, but a little white and shaken, she found Madame on the doorstep.

There was, it seemed, the tour of a musical comedy going out in the autumn. There was a solo dancer wanted. Madame believed she could get it for Daisy. Would Miss Howard consider a tour?

"Grand experience! grand experience! grand experience! Find her feet! find her feet! find her feet!"

Rose, thinking to herself that Daisy's feet were the one part of her she didn't need to find, considered the question.

"A tour; it might be a very good idea. Take them away all the autumn, while people were viewing the house. Of course, there was Mr. Carfax with his tests and operations. Still, that could wait until after Christmas, no one else knew about all that. The question was Tania, for Maimie of course was working and couldn't leave town."

Madame thought she could probably get Tania fixed as Daisy's understudy, she couldn't promise more, there were some children in the show, but Tania fell between two stools; too tall for a real child's part, too small for the chorus.

After a fortnight's suspense for Daisy, she was engaged. Rose signed a contract for her. Rehearsals were to begin in a month. They would open in Birmingham. Daisy was so excited, she could hardly eat or sleep. To get away in term-time. To start off as a solo dancer, not just one of a large troupe like the others were. To have her photograph taken in every sort of position, and two large frames made for the photographs, with Daisy Whichart printed on the bottom in large black letters. And a travelling case made for the frames, with "Daisy Whichart," in gigantic white letters, written across it. She liked the envy of the other girls at the academy. She liked even better the real interest of the girls at school. At the academy they expected her to get a good job; she'd always been a show pupil, and although they were envious, they were used to solo dancers. But at school, when she told her friends that she wouldn't be coming back in the autumn because she was going on tour, they thought it quite the most exciting thing they had ever heard. Only twelve, and touring all over England, dancing in a different theatre every week. What a glorious life; so different from their own humdrum existences. Some people had all the luck!

Tania was engaged to understudy Daisy. She felt

utterly crushed. She knew she would loathe touring. She would like the everlasting moving about, but travelling with all those people in the show! She'd hate that. She was humiliated by understudying Daisy. She knew that Daisy was a far better dancer. In fact, that she would never make a solo dancer at all. She could do all the steps, she had good technique, but she was uninspired, she had none of Daisy's artistry, and abandon. She felt ashamed of herself at school, and at the academy. She kept telling herself, what did it matter anyway? She wouldn't be dancing much longer; as soon as she was old enough, she'd get a mechanic's licence, and work at something she really could do. But she couldn't blind herself to the fact that it did matter, that they were all saying: "Oh, she's no good, got to understudy her younger sister." Then, as if this understudy business wasn't enough, there was Mr. Williams going away. The only person who liked the same things as she did. The only person who could see how very little this dancing business really mattered, and could be relied on to make you see it too, when a combination of events robbed you of your sense of proportion. Oh, life was miserable, the things it did to you. Not just one thing at a time, but two or three awfulnesses all at once.

CHAPTER 10

The musical comedy company left London on a Sunday morning. Maimie, Nannie, and Violet came to see their family off. Nannie very worried at losing sight of her children. She would have preferred to travel with them herself, leaving Rose in London. But Rose had insisted on going. She had no idea what touring might be like. She must see for herself what the conditions were.

"Now take care of yourselves, do," said Nannie, "and change into your woollies as soon as ever it gets cold. Gets cold before you can say 'knife' in them towns up north."

Maimie looked at them rather enviously. She had never been on tour. Never been away except for Sussex. It all looked rather fun. The carriages marked with their names. The fuss and bustle, such a lot of talking and laughing. Then all the journeys they would have. The places they would see. Different rooms. New ones every Sunday. They were even going as far as Scotland. Oh yes, they were lucky. London wasn't going to be much fun. That big house empty except for herself, Nannie, Violet, and Cook. People coming round to look at it all the time, and perhaps the trouble of packing for a move. And Dolly going to America almost at once. She wished he'd take her with him; she didn't believe her show would run over Christmas. Dolly was funny lately; didn't seem to think it would be a good idea. All the bother of looking for work. She hated bother. No bothers going on tour. She almost wished she were going with them. Still, the men didn't look up to much; looked poor. No good knowing men who hadn't got money.

Rose took her hand and kissed her:

"Take care of yourself, darling. Don't stop up too late, and do everything that Nannie tells you."

Maimie returned the kiss.

"Poor darling, she must be going ga-ga. How old does she think I am? Three?"

The tour did well. Daisy enjoyed every minute of it. Her dancing was a great success. She was the pet of the company. She looked forward all day to the evenings in the theatre; this, in spite of the fact that she found the rest of the day fun. She did her lessons with the other children in the show. She liked that, because she was far ahead of them and she didn't mind Miss Dene, the governess who travelled with them, and looked after the other children. She liked the afternoons when Rose was well enough, and took them to explore the town, that was most amusing. Then after tea she had a rest. Even that wasn't a bore, for Rose was reading the most exciting book to her. Yes, the stage was a gorgeous life. The conversation of the others hadn't prepared her for what fun it would be. Maimie had always quite liked her work, especially at the beginning, but even she had complained bitterly at times. As for Tania! To hear her talk you would think it was the most awful work in the world. Daisy never reasoned things out, so she supposed vaguely that it made a difference being a principal, and perhaps tour was more fun than London. Of course Tania wasn't really enjoying this tour. But that was because she was understudying; everyone said that was terribly boring work.

Far from "really enjoying" the tour, Tania was detesting every minute of it. She so loathed the professional rooms where they stayed. And the little back streets the rooms were in. On Sunday evenings she would be so crushed by the woolly mats, the aspidistras, the enlargements of the landladies' family, the curious smell of old food and dirty carpets, the shiny horsehair sofa with the stuffing coming out and all the springs broken; the unspeakable bathroom, the bedrooms with the wallpaper hanging in shreds, the sheets and blankets that needed a nervous examination before you dared get between them; the street outside, with its dreary row of equally awful little houses, the dirty paper blowing up the gutter, the noisy children playing over the drains; that, try as she would, she couldn't hide it. When Rose, herself loathing it, tried to cheer her up, she could only say:

"I'm sorry, Howdy. It's because I can't help hoping. All the day in the train I keep saying, 'Oh, it can't be as bad this time.' Then we arrive. Same awful smell. Same awful landlady. Same awful photographs. I just feel I can't bear it!"

Rose was able to bear with the tour, knowing how convenient it was being. "Young Mr. Bray" had succeeded in selling the house. He got rather more for it than he had hoped, because a syndicate was buying it, and the two houses next to it, to make a small hotel. Rose's was the middle one. She hated to think of her house as just the middle bit of a second-rate hotel, but there it was, off her hands for ever. She ought to be thankful.

"Young Mr. Bray" had also found them a flat, not far from the Cromwell Road, close to South Kensington Station. Nannie wrote that she thought she had better come north, to take charge of the children, and Rose come south for the move, to decide which furniture she would keep, and which sell, and how she wanted the rooms arranged. But Rose was not interested in the move. The house in the Cromwell Road had been her home, her life. The flat was for the children. "I leave the choice of rooms and furniture to Maimie," she wrote. "Store all the rest of the furniture till I come home." "Young Mr. Bray" urged her in several letters to come south at least for a weekend, to look the flat over before she signed the lease. But she answered, "No. If Maimie and Nannie think it will do, I shall think so too."

There was only one thing she would have liked, and that was to say good-bye to Cook. They wouldn't need her in the flat, and certainly couldn't afford her. She had been with Rose since the days of the Brigadier. She couldn't visualise life without her. And now that she was going, she couldn't even say good-bye.

They all wrote, Rose enclosing a cheque. Tania and Daisy sent a clock, which they had bought themselves out of their pocket-money. It was green enamel, and they thought it exquisite. So did Cook. She wrote to each of them, difficult, inexpressive letters, but one thing was clear, she refused to say good-bye. She should take a place in London, where she could come and look them up on her day out.

As the tour went on, Rose's health got worse, She said nothing about it to the children, but she gradually dropped the habit of taking them out in the afternoons, and handed them over to Miss Dene, who took them about with the other four children.

Miss Dene was a thin little person, with such a passion to rise above the conditions of her rather dull life, that it amounted to a creed. She would have enjoyed being a Christian Martyr. "This," she would have said with a bright smile, as she was stoned, or burned, or otherwise finished off, "may be unpleasant, but don't let us complain, there is a jolly side to it if we only look!" Not having lived in the days of Christian Martyrs, she brought her bright smile and "jolly side" creed to the minor martyrdoms. She always smiled. The more devastatingly depressing the weather, or the town she found herself in, the brighter shone her smile, the "jollier" she found things. As the rain splashed on the railway-carriage windows, on a long Sunday journey with Wigan as its objective, or when one of the children was sick over her only fur coat, she glowed! She effulged! She tried to instil her attitude towards life into her charges. In order to prove how "jolly" even the most unlikely town could be, she insisted on their visiting the local beauty spots. Whatever the weather she dragged them from castles to churches, and from churches to Elizabethan houses, and where there were none of these, she took them for a long tram ride, finishing with a "jolly" ramble in the country.

The children one and all detested beauty spots. Their idea of a really good afternoon was to be taken to the pictures. Even Tania, who might have enjoyed the walks, and taken a cursory interest in the churches and castles, wilted before such enthusiasm.

The long evenings in the theatre, which were a rapture to Daisy, were particularly trying to Tania. She was supposed to sit in Daisy's room, reading or sewing. If Rose came with them, it wasn't so bad, she brought a pack of cards, and they spent the evenings gambling for halfpennies. But Rose frequently left them to Miss Dene, especially when, as often happened, they all lived in the same street, and could therefore be dropped on the way home. On those nights Tania was a real example of the adage about "Satan finding mischief." She found it difficult to read in the theatre; even the most thrilling flying aces and motor fiends couldn't hold her attention. People kept talking to her, kept running in and out. Daisy couldn't find her dresser, and wanted hooking or buttoning. So as she detested sewing, she got into the habit of lolling in a chair, yawning her head off, and driving Daisy and the dresser distracted by getting crosser and crosser as the night wore on. She was so bad-tempered one night that she reduced Daisy to tears, whereupon Miss Dene took her to sit in the other dressing-room with the rest of the children. This was a hopeless failure and caused so noisy a quarrel that an infuriated assistant stage-manager came up to complain. After that she was moved back again to Daisy's room. Then quite by accident, and to everyone's relief, she found a friend. Daisy tore one of her stage dresses, and Tania, glad of something to do, offered to take it up to the wardrobe-mistress. She had never met Miss Poll before, who was a person of great dignity and importance, and not one as a general rule to take an interest in any children who might be in the show with which she was connected, especially one who was only an understudy. But as it happened, on the night Tania brought up Daisy's frock, she was badly in need of a confidante. Her trouble was a leading lady.

"Imagine it, dear," she said, examining the tear. " 'oo is she? That's what I say. Pantomime boy as was. And now only playing second lead for all 'er airs. She sends for me to 'er dressing-rom; and mind you, I'd never 'ave gone, only she sends Mr. Errol up for me. 'Come quick,' 'e says to me, 'she's in one of 'er worst!' Down I comes. She says to me, 'Did h'I or did h'I not tell you to make me new knickers for the second act?' 'You did,' I says, 'and when I've time I'm going to.' With that she screams out, 'You'll make them now, you bitch,' and she takes one leg in each 'and, tears 'er knickers in 'alf, and throws 'em on the floor before me face. Up I gets and walks out all dignified. No one could say I didn't act genteel. 'You Meadow Lady,' was all I ses. And I leaves the knickers lyin' in two 'alves on the floor. Up I goes to my room, and two minutes later up comes Mr. Errol. 'e looks quite white, po'r fellow. 'Oh Polly,' 'e says, 'for the Lord's sake mend them knickers, for she's 'avin' 'ysterics, an' says she won't go on.' I says, 'Either she goes on with them legs split in 'alf or not at all, for not one stitch do I put in them to-night. Insulted I've bin.' 'Oh come,' 'e says all friendly like, 'I know she's a terror, but you're a dear. Sew 'em together. There's a big 'ouse, and the understudy's lousy.' Well, I gives in an' I sews 'em up. But I 'ope I made 'em that tight that she splits the seat on the stage. Dirty bitch!"

Tania adored Miss Poll, who would talk by the hour, and she loved listening. Miss Poll had been for five years dresser to a musical comedy star.

"Lovely job that was, dearie—Ruthie was a nice little thing—but I always knew how it would end. 'Ruthie's the girl for the Lords,' I often ses to mother. And sure enough she snips one—'e sends up 'is card one night—would she join 'is party for supper? 'Go down', she says to me, 'an' give 'im the once-over—if 'e looks all right say I'll come'. Down to the stage-door I goes—what a boy!—not so outrageous good-looking, but lovely eyes—I says, 'Is you Lord 'enry?' 'Yes,' 'e says, and pops a pound note in me 'and. 'Tell 'er I'm all right,' 'e says. Upstairs I goes. 'You 'urry, dearie,' I ses to Ruthie, 'an' if 'e ses snip, you say snap, and you'll find yourself in Easy Street.' Well, that was the beginning, but she took an awful while to make up 'er mind—then just as I thought she was going to do it, she 'as an offer for America, an' believe me she took it! 'All right,' says 'is Lordship, 'you go! I'm tired of 'anging about—been running about after you for a year, I 'ave—you go to America, an' I'll try an' find someone who won't take so long making up their mind.' That done it! Broke her contrac' she did! What a wedding! They gave me a 'ole new rig-out—pink it was—smart pink 'at an' all—an' a nice little fur—an' the Lord 'isself see that I 'ad a button'ole. At the reception 'e brings me a glass of champagne. 'Polly,' 'e ses, 'drink our 'ealths, for you brought us together!' Which in a manner of speakin' I did—for if I'd come back an' said 'Na-poo' that night 'e first sends up 'is card, she'd never 'ave seen 'im. They tries to get me to come as a maid or somethin' at one of 'is 'ouses in the country. But I wouldn't go, I should miss the theatre, dear, I likes the smell of grease-paint of a night-time. Then I've me father an' mother back in Deptford, they likes me to be at 'ome, I've only come on tour this once just to oblige, an' because they've promised me dressin' in London at Christmas."

One evening, Tania discovered Miss Poll laboriously writing a letter.

"It's to my mother, dear. Almost Armistice Day, so I'm sendin' 'er a bit to buy a wreath."

"A wreath?" Tania was amazed. Wreaths on Armistice Day meant somebody you were fond of had been killed in the war. She had never connected Miss Poll with any sort of tragedy, she was always cheerful and amusing; of course she got angry sometimes, but that soon passed over. "Had you a brother killed in the war?" she asked sympathetically.

"Well, I 'ad, and I 'adn't in a manner of speakin'. My brother 'e went to France in '14—'ad a good job

104

tailorin' up till then. Smart 'e was. We used to laugh an' call 'im a waxwork. Well, it turns out that the man 'e'd worked for been a German, nice little chap 'e was, an' acourse 'e couldn't 'elp what 'e was born, but for all that 'e 'ad to go. So when the war was over there was my brother without a job. 'e tried everywhere, but 'e couldn't seem to get any work nohow. You see 'e'd grown that big in the army, none of 'is clothes seemed to fit 'im—'e was downright shabby. There wasn't a job goin' 'e didn't try for. 'e got little things sometimes —temporary—one year 'e was Father Christmas for one of the shops—'e didn't 'alf 'ate that. Dad was only doin' odd days then, business bein' slack. Course there was my dressin' money. We done what we could, never let 'im go out without a copper or two in 'is pocket, if it was only to 'ave somethin' to shake. But 'e did 'ate bein' that shabby—for 'e'd always been so smart. Didn't seem right some'ow. Then one day 'e comes in—very low 'e was. 'e sits down an' takes off 'is boots. I give 'im a cigarette I'd been savin' for 'im. 'Think I'll smoke it in the yard,' 'e says. 'What!' says mother, 'you never goin' out there without your boots!' 'Sorry, ma,' 'e says, an' pulls 'em on again. Outside 'e goes—an' we 'ears a bang—I runs out, an' there 'e's been an' gone an' shot 'isself. Mother took it bad. But she's getting' better now. But she does like to put a wreath on the Cenotaph on an Armistice Day. Of course it ain't got no right to be there, but what I says is, the other boys won't mind."

Tania was startled; this story presented a new facet to life. Such an awful thing to happen, and yet Miss

Poll took it in her stride, as it were. She'd never mentioned it before, it didn't seem to over-cloud her life, she was always most jovial. Could things like that happen to other people? To her for instance? Could the people you loved die, and after a time you be gay and amusing as though nothing had happened? She shivered.

"Goose run over your grave?" asked Miss Poll.

Sometimes Miss Poll would question Tania about herself. The two sisters were so unlike, they made her curious. They were so obviously a cut above the other children. Then Miss Howard, so very presentable a guardian. How did she come to have possession of the children? Very queer it all was.

"You an' Daisy do this for fun, most like?"

"Fun!" Tania was staggered. Would anyone do it for fun? "I wouldn't think it fun even if I was Daisy, but goodness knows, nobody would understudy for fun. It's the foullest job in the world."

"Never mind, dearie, things is bound to improve. You'll be a star one day perhaps."

"Oh my goodness, I do hope not."

"Well, it's worth working for, dear. Look at the money they makes."

Money! Here was a new thought. Stars of course made money. And when they'd made it, they could spend it any way they liked. Have cars, aeroplanes, anything. She went to Rose as soon as she got home. Did Rose think she would ever do really well on the stage? She was very small, couldn't she specialise in acrobatics? Rose was puzzled. Tania ambitious? She

106

supposed she was feeling her position as Daisy's understudy.

"I don't really think it's your line, darling. I don't think you've got a stage temperament. I thought later on I'd have you trained for something else."

"What else?"

Rose was vague

"Well, perhaps a secretary, or you might run something, a library or—or perhaps you could work in a shop—very nice people work in shops nowadays."

"What would I earn?"

Rose had the haziest ideas. She thought round about three pounds a week was what most girls earned.

Three pounds a week! Why, Maimie'd been earning more than that for ages, and she was only chorus.

"One couldn't save much on that, could one?" she asked anxiously.

No. Rose supposed one couldn't. But one could manage, and it might be interesting work. After all, that was something.

Something, but not much, thought Tania, How, if one has no talent, and no money, does one do what one wants in life? Of course one might marry, that wasn't much of a chance, and a rotten prospect anyway. One would presumably only live once. If there was another world it was probably a boring affair devoted to church music. Surely, then, it was up to you to get what you wanted out of this life. But how? All that bunk people talked. "Life is what you make of it." "The fault, dear Brutus, is not in our stars——" All that muck! Daisy would probably make money because she really could dance. She hadn't worked any harder than she had, but just had the gift. Maimie, too, would probably have what she wanted in life. She hadn't any special gift, unless making men like you was a gift, but she had the right temperament. She didn't mind hurting other people to get what she wanted. Things didn't worry her somehow. She didn't lie awake fussing, fussing, because she'd hurt Howdy, because Howdy might die, and then it would be too late to explain how very much one had cared really, even if one had never managed to say so. Maimie would hurt Howdy at any time if it suited her book. But she never cared, never worried. Obviously that was the right temperament to have if you wanted to get on. I wish I'd had those sort of parents who had money, or who left me money. That was the kind of luck to strike in life. "Not in our stars." God! what a lie.

Towards the end of the tour Rose's health grew worse. She made an excuse to the children that she must go to town on business, and she handed them over to Miss Dene.

The rest of the tour was a nightmare. Even Daisy hated it. Living in rooms with Howdy and Tania had been fun. Living in rooms with Miss Dene, Annie, Dot, Gloria, and Babs, was a very different matter. As for Tania, she sank into a state of unalleviated gloom. She felt desperately nervous. Why had Howdy suddenly gone to London? She didn't for one moment believe in the "business." Was Maimie ill? and they weren't being told? Was Nannie leaving? Was there something wrong with Howdy herself? Something awful was going to happen, she felt it with every nerve.

The continual aggravation of being crushed into small rooms with all the other children didn't help matters. Their endless chattering and giggling reduced her almost to hysteria. She was insufferable to live with, unbearably bad-tempered. Even Miss Dene, interested though she was in the girl, failed to see any "jolly" side to her during those weeks after Rose left.

Only with Miss Poll did Tania feel at all herself. She made her feel that even if something awful was going to happen, she'd be able to bear it. Her chatter had the effect on Tania that cold water has on a sprained ankle.

"What's worriting you, child? You look frayed to a fiddlestring."

"I don't know."

"Maybe you're missin' Miss 'oward?"

"Oh, I don't know."

"Well, I expects you finds it noisy all them other children under your feet all day?"

"Perhaps."

"Well, what I ses is, never worry! I ses that to mother whenever things looks bad. An' I've always been right. Father loses 'is job. 'What we goin' to do now?' says mother, fussin' terrible. 'Don't fuss,' I says—'it won't 'elp you if thin's is bad, an' like as not somethin' will turn up, then you've 'ad all that fussin' for nothin'!' An' sure enough somethin' usually does.

Mother gets a bit of washin' or somethin'. Mind you, we been fortunate. As sure as ever father's out of work, I'm workin', an' if my show comes to an end, 'e's sure to 'ave a job. 'It's all wrong to fuss,' I says to mother; born lucky, that's what we are!"

The tour finished in the middle of December. It sleeted, off and on, during the last weeks, and there was a biting east wind. Daisy took to long gaiters. Tania put on every warm garment she possessed, but she was permanently perished with the cold. She looked smaller and thinner, even than usual; her always yellow skin, even yellower. The winter was deplorably unbecoming to her. The very last week they were in Glasgow. There had been snow, but it had become piles of grey filth in the gutters. The wind was blustery; it seemed to sweep from the clouds heavy with ice, career madly down the streets adding grit to its burden of cold, in order to fling itself unpleasantly at the miserable pedestrians.

On the last night here was a telegram at the theatre for Miss Dene. She called Tania.

"You must go back to the rooms, and pack your own and Daisy's things. I am to send you both down on tonight's train. I'll find out if any of the others are going who could travel with you."

"Why have we to go?"

Miss Dene swallowed the story she had intended to tell of a sudden contract for Daisy. Tania's eyes were not eyes to lie to. They were terrified, but they expected the truth.

"It's Miss Howard, dear, she's had an operation.

110

She wants to see you."

Back in the rooms, hurriedly throwing their things into the boxes, Tania's most dominant feeling was relief. So it had come. It couldn't well be worse. Howdy was going to die. After several weeks, during which a formless anxiety had lain under her heart until it caused an actual physical ache which could be alleviated by pressing her hand on it, the arrival of the bad news was relief. It removed the pain. The new pain hurt in quite a different way; a way that made you feel brave, determined to face things. The sort of unknown terror which had hung over her lately had had quite the opposite effect; it had sapped her courage, made a coward of her.

They arrived in London early on Sunday morning. Nannie, red-eyed, met them.

"It's Miss Howard, dears. She's been ill for some time, but she only gave in to it a week ago. They operated. They said she'd left it too late, but they thought it was worth a try——"

Nannie remembered a promise to Rose. She said hurriedly: "Anyway, she's doin' fine, but she was worryin' about you two, so I thought I'd send that telegram and get you home as quick as I could.

"When can we see her?" Tania asked.

"You an' Maimie is goin' round to see her as soon as I've 'ad you back at the flat an' given you somethin' to eat, an' you've 'ad a nice warm."

"I shall go too," said Daisy. "If Howdy's worrying, she'd better see us both, then she can see how well we are.

"It's Tania an' Maimie as she asked for special."

"That's because she thought I'd be tired, but I'm not, so I shall go too. I want to see darling Howdy. I shall take her some flowers."

"Young Mr. Bray" had found a cheap but well-run little nursing-home.

Rose lay flat on her back. Such an incredibly changed, yellow Rose. The children were shocked into silence by her appearance. In spite of the most gnawing pain, she had refused to have a drug injected that morning, until she had seen the children. She managed a smile.

"Well, babes. Hullo! Daisy, I wasn't expecting you. It's Maimie and Tania. But I'm glad to see you, darling." She felt feebly under her pillow, and produced two Bibles. "This is going to make you laugh. When you two were born———"

As she told them the story of the books, she turned her eyes first to Maimie and then to Tania.

Tania licked her lips. They were so dry, it was difficult to speak.

"Why are we to have them now?"

Rose turned to her. A look of perfect understanding passed between them. Out loud she said:

"I ought to have given them to you before, but I've always been so busy, I forgot. But listen, darlings, don't use these addresses unless things are very bad. After all, your mothers suffered terribly when they gave you up." A little smile quivered at the corner of her mouth as she looked at Maimie. "They were young. I asked to keep you, persuaded them against

112

their wills not to ruin their chances in life. They may be married now, have other children. Your sudden arrival might be most awkward. So lock the Bibles away, unless things go very wrong."

A nurse came in. Rose, who felt that pain was getting the upper hand of her, told the children they must go.

"We'll come again to-morrow, Howdy darling," said Daisy cheerfully, as she kissed her good-bye.

"I promise I'll never use my old Bible unless you advise it. I'm afraid I'm not the kind of daughter a long-lost mother would exactly leap at." Maimie forced a laugh to get herself out of the room without breaking down.

Tania just kissed her good-bye. She had nothing to say.

CHAPTER 11

Rose died that afternoon.

Tania and Daisy were sleeping after their night in the train. Maimie was lying on the sofa in the sitting-room, trying to alter a hat. The 'phone bell rang. She jumped to her feet.

"No, my lamb," said Nannie, taking the receiver from her, "better leave it to me."

Tania came in.

"Wasn't that the telephone?"

There was a pause, then Nannie said into the mouthpiece:

"Thank you, I'll tell them. Very peaceful. I understand."

Tania gripped hold of her.

"Nannie! Oh Nannie!"

Maimie turned white.

"Not Howdy?"

Unseen, Daisy came in at the door. Nannie nodded assent to Maimie. She tried to find her voice, then said in a whisper:

"Yes. 'Alf an 'our ago."

Daisy, terrified by their faces, shook her.

"What is it? What happened half-an-hour ago?"

Maimie broke down and cried:

"It's Howdy, she's dead."

"Young Mr. Bray" came round to see them that evening. He rang half-a-dozen times before he could

114

get an answer. Then a very swollen-eyed Maimie opened the door. He patted her on the shoulder.

"Let me see, you must be Maimie. I am Mr. Bray."

"Oh, how glad I am to see you. Tania won't speak. Daisy keeps on being sick. And Nannie does nothing but cry."

"Young Mr. Bray" took command. As his A.D.C. he chose Tania, who, though she hadn't said a word, seemed to have kept her wits. He put her in a taxi, and sent her to his housekeeper for champagne. The champagne revived them all wonderfully. Daisy stopped being sick. Nannie and Maimie stopped crying. Nannie even recovered sufficiently to cook some eggs. Not till they had all eaten, and thanks to the food and champagne looked a shade more cheerful, did he venture on the business that had brought him. He had come to arrange about the funeral. Wouldn't it be much better to let him go to it alone? There was no need for them to go, they'd only upset themselves. The children were shocked. Not go to Howdy's funeral? Gracious! who should go if they didn't? They all said so at once. He quickly capitulated. Of course they must go if they felt like that; he had only thought to save them needless pain. Then there was the future to discuss. Not to-night, of course. But he thought the sooner the better. He would come round again to-morrow morning. Finally he persuaded them it was time for bed.

"I shall sit here till you all reach the pyjama stage, then one of you must come down and let me out."

Maimie giggled hysterically.

"You'll sit there for ever if you wait for that. Nannie doesn't wear pyjamas."

The next morning Maimie woke up suddenly. Tania was sitting on her bed. She spoke urgently:

"You know 'Young Mr. Bray' is coming back today——"

"Yes," Maimie yawned, "to discuss the future."

"Well, we ought to make up our minds first——"

"What about?"

"Well, first there's our Bibles, what are you going to do about yours?"

"I can tell you that in one. Burn it."

"Gracious! Why? When Howdy kept it for you all these ages."

"If Howdy could hear what we're saying, she'd be damn glad. She had to give me my mother's name and address; it was only fair, but she knew I'd never use it. Do you know that my mother lived in a manse? That's Scotch for a vicarage! Now I ask you! Can you see me making the pretty entrance up the moss-grown garden path, clutching my Bible, and greeting a perfectly strange female with: 'Mother, I'm your little Maimie'? No! That's cut for the second house."

"I shall keep mine always." Tania hugged her knees to her chin. "I don't suppose I'll ever use it— but I like the feeling it's there. Still, it wasn't the Bibles I really wanted to talk about. It's us, all three of us. Do you suppose 'Young Mr. Bray' will try and separate us?"

"Why on earth should he? Here's the flat. There's room for all of us. In fact, now Howdy's——"

116

"I don't believe Howdy ever legally adopted us," Tania interrupted, "there was a sort of hitch over our stage licences because of it. We don't belong to anyone now. Even if Howdy did properly adopt us in the end, we aren't the sort of belongings you leave people in wills. Howdy only kept us out of charity; no one else is likely to."

"I don't believe it. Whichart must have left some money to support us."

"Well, we shall soon know whether he did or didn't; the point is, what line are we going to take? I'm going to fetch Daisy."

Tania found Daisy even more lethargic than Maimie.

"I suppose Nannie will look after us. Somebody always looks after children, they aren't just left."

Tania was exasperated.

"That's all you know. Children are often left. And anyhow you're the only child here, Maimie and I are women. But what I want is that whatever happens we all stick together. I don't believe we've any money. We haven't any family. We haven't even a real name. But there is us three. It's heaps better to be three than one. Now I swear that whatever job I get, I'll give all I earn towards keeping a home for us. And I shall tell 'Young Mr. Bray' so this morning. What about you, Maimie?"

Maimie felt slightly embarrassed. It was very unlikely she'd always want to live at home. Even when Rose was alive, she had often played with the thought of getting away on her own. So much more freedom, no one to bother you with questions. Still, if it was true there wasn't going to be any money, it would certainly need them all to help if they were to keep a roof over their heads. She was the most consistent wage-earner, it would be dirty to back out now.

"I promise to pay my whack towards the house and everything——"

"And you, Daisy?" Tania looked at her anxiously, was she too going to be half-hearted?

"Every bit I earn, of course." Daisy needed no persuasion. "But you do remember, Tania, that I'm licensed, and one-third has to go in the bank. But as soon as I'm fourteen, I'll give every penny."

Tania was dissatisfied. Did they care? If 'Young Mr. Bray' suggested something else, would they calmly give in? Nannie interrupted the meeting.

"Breakfast," she announced. "An' since none of you is dressed, you'll 'ave to 'ave it in your dressing-gowns."

"Young Mr. Bray" saw Nannie first. He told her that although Rose had left her guardian to the children, there was so little money that he thought they had better not attempt to keep the flat. Daisy could go to an inexpensive boarding-school. Tania and Maimie might live in a hostel—— He rambled on, testing her, waiting for what he was sure she would say. He didn't get very far, when Nannie burst out, just as he had expected:

"Not keep on the flat! No home indeed! Blessed lambs. Live in a 'ostel indeed! Send Daisy to a boardin'-school! And for why? 'aven't we got this flat?

118

And all the children workin' off an' on. An' come to the worst there's me savin's."

"Young Mr. Bray" objected. They hadn't got the flat. But they had got about two hundred a year from the sale of the house in the Cromwell Road.

"That will pay the rent and——" He hesitated. "Your wages."

"My wages is my business. You pay the rent. An' I'll manage on what's over, an' on what they earns. As far as may be things can go on as before. Tania an' Daisy can go back to school, an' to Madame's of an afternoon. An' when I says I can't manage, it's time to talk of breakin' up their 'ome."

He saw Maimie next. He was amazed to find how lovely she was when her nose wasn't swollen with crying. He told her just where they stood and of Nannie's wish to try to carry on.

"Well, young lady, you are the eldest, and you are working. Do you approve? Are you prepared to help?"

"I'll tell you exactly what I think, and what I'll do, and then we'll know where we are."

Her directness reminded him ludicrously of her father.

"I think Nannie's quite right to keep on the flat if she can. The kids must live somewhere. It's all right for me, I'm old enough to get a place of my own. But they're only children, they must have a home. As regards helping, I always gave Howdy twenty-five shillings a week when I was working and nothing when I wasn't. Now I shall go on doing the same, only I'll pay all the time, whether I'm working or not."

"My dear child, how?"

"Don't you worry. I shall."

"Forgive me. I'm an old man, and you probably consider me a prosy old bore. But I knew and liked your father, and I had the deepest respect for Miss Howard. She left Mrs. Rigg—Nannie," he added apologetically—"your guardian, with me as a watchdog in the background, as it were. On all these counts perhaps you'll bear me in mind, and remember that, old bore though I may be, I shall be glad to give you advice if ever you should need it."

Tania came in surly and tongue-tied with nervousness. He explained the situation to her, but he did not ask for her approval. She was a child. Children did what they were told.

"As far as possible, everything will go on as before. You and Daisy will go back to school and to the Dancing Academy, and if you are fortunate enough to obtain employment, it will be a great help towards the household expenses."

"Of course I'll give Nannie all I earn. But I think it would be better to train me for something else instead of sending me back to school."

"Train you for what?"

"Well, something——" Should she tell him, was he the sort to understand?—"something to do with machinery."

"Young Mr. Bray" laughed. He didn't understand her. He took her for a tomboyish young person still at the stage of wanting to be an engine-driver.

"No, no, machinery's not for little girls."

Without a word she left the room.

He sat Daisy on his knee. He hoped she'd make a great dancer.

"I hope I'll make a lot of money to help keep us."

He stroked her red curls.

"Little heads shouldn't worry about things of that sort."

He made a mental note to order her some chocolates on the way home.

They drove to the funeral in "Young Mr. Bray's" car. They might be poor, economy might be the grimmest necessity, but Nannie said:

"There's times when savin's wrong—an' mournin's one of 'em".

So it was a party of crows who stood round Rose's grave. It was a heavenly morning. The sky was an almost royal blue, there was a delicious nip of frost in the air. There were lots of wreaths; they were all of chrysanthemums, mostly the golden-brown kind. They gave out that curious pungent autumnal smell. Maimie and Daisy cried bitterly, more because they had reached the last lap of the days of overwhelming depression than because the shining box sliding into the earth upset them. They had got used to the fact that Rose was dead, she would never come back. A shiny box couldn't really make things worse.

For the first time since Rose had died, Tania was happy. The glory of the morning got into her veins. She had a sure feeling that Rose was happy and was trying to tell her so. She thought suddenly: "Heaven is like Sussex. All space. You feel quick all over. You can

121

move very fast."

That afternoon she bought herself some golden-brown chrysanthemums.

"Miss Extravagance," said Nannie, who was feeling cross after such a plethora of emotion.

"I know it's awful of me. But it's only for this once. I'll never buy myself flowers again."

She smelt them, and shut her eyes. She couldn't get the feeling quite—yes, there it was—the sharpness of the frost—the tang of the chrysanthemums—Howdy's happy—it's like Sussex.

Apart from a large wreath, Madame showed her sympathy by promptly finding Tania and Daisy work. She had already planned to take Daisy to a pantomime audition for a dancing part, she now tried really hard to fix Tania in the same show.

"Keep 'em together, keep 'em together, keep 'em together," she said to Nannie.

She succeeded. Daisy was engaged as a speciality child dancer. Tania was attached to a troupe of twelve children in the same show, "Madame Elise's Twelve Little Pumpkins," the pantomime being "Cinderella". She found herself terribly out of practice after her three and a half months' tour, during which she had scarcely worked at an exercise, and only lifelessly gone through Daisy's dances at the understudy rehearsals; she had to really slave to get herself sufficiently supple to get through the quite difficult steps required of her. Daisy, billed as "The Child Wonder", though infinitely more important, had a far easier time.

The pantomime ran well, and Daisy was a great

success. Hope ran high in the flat. After such wonderful notices as she had had, she might get a stupendous offer at any moment. No one was very hopeful of Tania getting work, she was at the plain stage, and had suddenly begun to grow very leggy, and her black clothes, which were all the winter clothes she possessed, were most unbecoming to her. Both boredom with her work, and depression, for she missed Rose abominably, told on her health, she looked sallow, she stooped, and her hair hung lankly.

"Miss Plain I said first time I seen her," said Nannie to Maimie, "an' I was about right."

But the pantomime came to an end, and no one wanted either of the children. Madame tried hard. Nannie, Tania and Daisy eagerly watched for every post, and flew to answer every telephone call. But no one wrote or rang up. Tania was efficient, and Daisy quite brilliant, but children dancers simply were not wanted. Then in April, Maimie's revue, which had been doing quite well, suddenly flickered and died. Dolly Kismet was still in America. She said that of course she'd easily get another job. It didn't need Dolly to find it for her, she was known quite a bit now, it would be quite simple. But there was only one new musical show coming on; she went to the audition for that, but she was not engaged; the music was elaborate, they wanted their girls to be singers more than dancers; Maimie's voice was not up to the standard.

While the children had worked, Nannie had tried to save. Tania had handed over the whole of her salary

123

every week. But then she obviously needed new clothes, the money ought to go on those. There had been two-thirds of Daisy's far larger salary coming in, but Daisy too needed new clothes. Nannie decided to try and run the house on Maimie's twenty-five shillings. The children could make their present clothes do for another month; she would hold on to their savings for a bit anyway, and perhaps she wouldn't need to spend them, something might turn up. Tania, in spite of "Young Mr. Bray's" dictum, had refused to go back to school. She explained her reasons to Nannie.

"I know the fees aren't much, but then I don't earn much. And what I do earn, you need just to keep me; I don't want to be kept by the others. I shall be sixteen this summer, it's not a bit too soon to leave, and you'll be glad of me to help you in the house."

So all the morning she worked in the flat. In the afternoons and part of the evening, she worked at the academy. But whether at housework or dancing, she kept turning her position over in her head. She ought to try for something else. Here she was nearly sixteen, and only working at Christmas. But if she took another job, a messenger girl for instance, she would be busy all day, and her dancing would get out of practice. She was trained as a dancer; in a few months, if she looked a little less plain, she might get into a grown-up chorus. Obviously she would earn more while she was working in the thing for which she was trained; unskilled labour didn't earn much. She was afraid to try for any other job, she had no idea what could be earned, and it would be awful if she went off on her own and got something to do, and then found Madame had a well-paid job for her if only she'd stopped on. Yet somebody must get a job. If they didn't, Nannie might have to ask for help from "Young Mr. Bray" ; that mustn't be. He would think they couldn't manage, he'd want to try something else. Tania could see quite clearly what she ought to do, she ought to have a talk with Madame.

Her thoughts always led to this point, but it was days before she could make up her mind to carry it out. She was terrified of Madame. She didn't know why, Madame had always been very kind, but there it was, she would rather have done almost anything than ask a favour of her. But at last, urged by Nannie's worried face, she took the plunge. She hung about nervously outside the office door. She looked plain and awkward. Her check romper didn't suit her long legs. She was too tall for socks, her nose and elbows looked blue, for it was cold in the passage. Madame, hurrying by, saw her.

"Well, Tania? Well, Tania? Well, Tania? What is it? What is it? What is it?"

Haltingly, Tania explained. She stressed no point. Madame knew Rose was dead, knew they needed the money. What she did not know was how much they needed it. Tania didn't say, but the way she said, "I must find work. Could you help me?" convinced Madame that there was urgency. She rang a bell. Muriel, the black-haired instructress, flew in.

"Tania too big, too big, too big. Pansy's Peaches,

125

Pansy's Peaches, Pansy's Peaches?"

"Stand up, Tania."

Tania turned anxious eyes on Muriel.

"No. She doesn't look more than thirteen, and Pansy's not fussy. But does she want another Peach?"

"Lucy leaving, Lucy leaving, Lucy leaving." Madame waved a hand in dismissal.

"You don't want to join the Peaches, do you?" asked Muriel curiously, when they got outside. "They aren't your style at all, and the dancing's awful. Just one-two-three hop. I should think you'd hate it."

"Well, I have to do something," answered Tania grumpily.

Pansy Daw was a music-hall star. She made a vast fortune at song-plugging. Dressed in the most startling creations, she sang her songs, repeating the choruses so many times that it was a certainty that even the least musically-minded member of the audience must leave the theatre humming them. To increase the effect, Pansy contracted yearly with Madame Elise for twelve children, twelve competent girls who could be guaranteed to beat out the metre with their feet whenever she herself was singing, and who would continue the good work of screaming out the songs if she herself should dance a few steps. She never knew the names of her twelve girls, she barely knew them by sight. Provided they could do their work, Madame could send whom she liked. It was not one of the picked jobs of the academy. The work was hard—music-halls—always twice nightly, and sometimes three performances a day. The standard of dancing required was very low, the girls were picked mainly because they were small for their ages. Although they were sent in charge of a matron, none of them were under fourteen and many of them a great deal older.

Tania was sent under the escort of Muriel to her first rehearsal. She found she scarcely knew the other eleven Peaches by sight. Her work was in a class far beyond theirs, and she had hardly spoken to them outside, for they belonged to the rougher and dirtier contingent of pupils. She sighed as she changed into her romper and shoes.

The work she found very easy, she could have done it in her sleep. What bored her were the clothes. They changed an incredible number of times in the short while their turn was on. She could have borne with it if there had been any reason in the changing, but as far as she could see, there was none. In pantomime you changed at least with some purpose; the principal boy sang about Old Madrid, and you appeared all ribbons and castanets. Or the principal girl sang about Lilac, and you came in at any rate dressed in mauve, if it was only as a mauve powder-puff. But not so with Pansy. When she sang about Dixie and coal-black mammies, you put on an Early Victorian frock or dressed up in yellow swansdown as a chicken. But when she sang about grandmamma's days, or the spring, then was the moment when you appeared as a coon, or in Hawaiian get-up. It was all most confusing, and even to Tania, whose taste was none too good, it appeared very inartistic. It was not till she had been with Pansy for quite a while, and rehearsed innumerable new numbers, that she realised that Pansy, who was a busy woman, had originally fixed the order in which the dresses were to be worn, and for no subsequent change of programme did she bother to alter it. She hadn't the time, she said, to be always fussing about.

Tania had her first solo part with Pansy. In one number, one of the children had to sing a chorus alone and unaccompanied. The Peaches were always changing, and the girl who had done this part left very suddenly. A hasty trial of voices proved that the remainder of the Peaches possessed more volume than tone; of the lot Tania was the most tuneful. She was quite unsuited, as the whole idea was that the singer should be very undersized with yellow curls, so that the audience could say: "What a little mite, can't be more than ten!" But owing to a shortage of the right type, and the fact that everyone was too busy to bother, she kept her solo for quite a time. This put an idea into her head.

She had all along taken a great interest in Pansy. She was fair, blue-eyed, and tall, with a perfect figure. But she couldn't dance. She couldn't sing. She couldn't produce. She had no imagination. But she could put a song across, and for that she earned a salary that would have enthralled a prime minister. She was followed everywhere by a nervous little husband, who was a musician both by taste and by profession. He conducted for her, it was his only claim to her attention. She had also an enormous car, a devoted maid, and a humble chauffeur. She glittered with jewels, she had magnificent furs. Tania would look at her spellbound. There was money if you liked! Earned by putting on one of the stupidest and crudest music-hall turns in England. And yet, thought Tania, she's worth every penny she earns. Why? Because when she gets hold of a song, its sale goes into millions. Now why couldn't I learn to do that? I'm sure I'm more intelligent than she is, and I can dance and she can't, and I can sing about as well, at least I suppose I can sing, else why have I got that solo? Of course I'm nowhere near as good-looking, but I may improve. It's worth thinking of. Why! in a year or two I'd earn enough to have several aeroplanes. She practised the art of putting over songs on her family. They complained bitterly. Maimie said:

"If you must be one of Pansy's Peaches, for God's sake don't let's have it at home. We shall have you doing it next: 'Toothy Tania and her Toddlers.'"

Maimie could not hear of any work. She continued to pay Nannie twenty-five shillings a week. She said she had savings. Tania was handing over her weekly wage, but she didn't earn a great deal, and by the time Madame had taken her commission, there wasn't much left; not much to a family all needing new clothes. Nannie found that there was never a week but she was faced with some unexpected expense. Daisy had toothache—three visits to the dentist. Tania's shoes needed soling and heeling, and they were scarcely home before Daisy's went through. Little things all the time, but preventing that pile of savings accumulating that Nannie considered necessary for their safety. She could not feel justified in buying new clothes. Tania and Daisy looked positively shabby.

"Maybe in the summer sales——" said Nannie hopefully.

Maimie alone was smart, and not only smart but happy. She missed Rose in her own way, but she had things to amuse her, which her sisters had not. Dolly's departure to America had depressed her at first, but she had pointed out to herself that he was not the only "kipper in the sea," there were others. Not, it was true, others with as much influence as Dolly, but others with just as much money! Still, all these were just casuals. "I must freeze on to something good soon," she thought. But she couldn't bring herself to bother, she was having a good time, going about with first one man, and then another. It was fun and there wasn't all that jealous stuff, none of that fussing as to where you'd been and whom with. Still, it would be a good thing to fix up something more permanent. Rose's death had given her a shake-up, made her feel how insecure life was. It was in this mood she met Herbert Rosen.

He was a Jew, but he had not been noticeably one for a long time. His father was a baronet, they'd made vast sums in manufacturing paper, and with the vast sums done a lot for the country. Thus the baronetcy.

Herbert had fallen in love with Maimie while she had been playing in the revue. She had no idea that she had taken his fancy, for he had made no sign. But he had watched her. He wanted to know if there was someone else. Then one night he met her at a supper-party. He arranged to meet her again. Not too soon, he didn't believe in rushing things. After their next meeting he sent chocolates; after the third, flowers; after the fourth, scents; and after the fifth, which was in his flat, she could have more or less what she liked.

He wanted to give her a flat. He wanted to feel he really owned her. To know she was there if he should want her. He hated possessions he couldn't lock up. He couldn't lock up Maimie. He never knew what she did when she wasn't with him. She said she went home, she said she lived with two sisters and an old nurse. That for a tale! Besides, if it were true, it was time she got away. Old nurse indeed!

Maimie was selfish, but she was large-hearted. As a rule in a conflict the selfishness won. But over the business of a flat, she behaved well. If she let Herbert take a flat for her, how about their home? And her promise to Tania? Her twenty-five shillings a week was a help. Of course Herbert was really paying that now, and would go on sending that, and more, to Nannie every week if only she could get away. She toyed with the thought for a moment, but she could see it would never work. Nannie might be a bit blind, but even she would think that arrangement rather queer, it would take a lot of explaining. No, for the present things must go on as they were.

"I'm sorry, Herbert darling, I'd just adore to have a little place of my own. But I must think of the others, my sisters, how would they manage without me?"

Herbert, though annoyed about the flat, was touched. "Perhaps there really are some sisters," he thought. He'd test her.

"How about bringing those sisters of yours to tea to-morrow—Rumpelmayers."

Tania and Daisy were staggered when Maimie handed on the invitation. Nannie was so impressed that she excused them from their dancing-class so that they might go. And spent the morning steaming and brushing their black coats.

"It's a shame you has to go shabby, disgracing us in front of Maimie's gentleman friend."

It was a grand afternoon. Herbert, meeting Nannie delivering her charges, insisted that she should stay to tea too. Money had been so scarce lately in the flat that the food had been what is known as "good plain". The sight of so many exquisite cakes was as water to the parched.

Tania, eyeing a confection of marron, said to Herbert:

"Shall we act natural, and make hogs of ourselves? Or shall we behave like little ladies?"

"Let's all be hogs," he said.

It was the gayest meal. Herbert felt quite conscience-stricken when he remembered that the object of the invitation was to spy on Maimie's family, and here he was being taken to their bosom, feeling one of them, pressing Nannie to take yet one more chocolate éclair, assuring Daisy that there were times when feeling sick was worth while.

Driving Maimie back to his flat, he felt ashamed of

himself. Almost as though he had stolen her out of the schoolroom. He hated to feel mean like that, so he gave her a cheque.

CHAPTER 12

Daisy had the chance of a job. A revue was coming on, there was to be a very elaborate all-English ballet. A principal dancer was wanted. Madame, full of ambition for her favourite, suggested Daisy. There would be an audition. Nannie, with yards of tarleton, refurbished a ballet dress, patched the toes of Daisy's best ballet shoes, and washed and darned the family's only pair of silk tights. Then a blow fell. Tania brought a message. Madame said she had written to ask if Daisy might dance at the audition, and her name had met with approval from no less a person than Leon Low. Leon Low was presenting the revue. He had seen Daisy dance in the pantomime. He remembered her. He had thought her brilliant, but he was afraid she was too young for what he wanted. He suggested that Madame should bring her round to his office, so that he could study her. He didn't want a child, the ballet wasn't written for a kid. Madame had explained all this to Tania, who was to explain it to Nannie, who would please dress Daisy for the appointment, in such clothes that she looked a good two years older than her age.

They had just got new clothes. Neat fawn coats, with straw hats to match. In the house there were two pounds. Nannie and Tania discussed the situation. Even if Daisy wore Tania's coat it was no good pretending it aged her two years. It was a schoolgirl's coat and looked it. Obviously what was wanted was something smart, a little cloche hat, and not just a loose coat, but something with a shape. Maimie must help, something of hers must be altered. Maimie, when she got in, agreed at once. She laid armloads of frocks and coats and hats on the bed. But Maimie was her mother's daughter, she was exceptionally tall. Daisy was a shrimp, she didn't look as though she was thirteen. She was still wearing socks, they were so convenient for a dancer. In Maimie's clothes, she looked, as Tania said:

"A tiny slice of lamb, trying to look like a whole leg of mutton."

Even with the addition of Tania's best stockings she still looked a baby.

"Something simple but doggy is what she needs," moaned Tania—"but simple dogginess costs money".

Maimie was really distressed, she eyed her clothes regretfully. Bad luck if the kid lost the job just for lack of the right clothes. Certainly in her own things she looked hopeless, no style or anything, just a schoolgirl. She told Herbert of their troubles. He was touched, and delighted to find that Maimie was really worried; he hadn't known she had so kind a heart. Besides, if the kid really did well, got away with a good job, there'd be no need for Maimie to live at home. He gave Maimie twenty-five pounds.

"Take it to the child, tell her any lies you like, but get her fitted out."

Maimie went home triumphant. At breakfast the next morning she produced the money.

135

"There, Nannie, that's for Daisy's clothes."

They all eyed the money incredulously. Two ten-pound notes, one five-pound note. Astonishing wealth. And Maimie throwing it on the table as if it were threepence!

"Where did you get all that?" Nannie asked suspiciously.

Maimie had her lie ready.

"Racing—I backed a horse."

"Racing!" Nannie was visibly relieved. "I don't 'old with 'orse racin', still I won't say as it won't come in very 'andy. An' very generous of you to spare it, I must say."

Daisy raced round the table and flung her arms round Maimie's neck.

"Oh, Maimie darling, thank you. It's adorable of you. I really may get that job now. Then the first thing I'll do is to pay you back."

Tania said nothing, but only Maimie noticed. Daisy and Nannie were too excited, discussing the spending of so enormous a sum.

After breakfast Tania got Maimie alone.

"Maimie, we can't take that money."

"Why the hell not?"

"Because it isn't fair."

"What isn't fair? I tell you I won it on a horse."

"Why tell lies to me? You know I know it wasn't a horse. Herbert gave it you. Or one of the other men you know."

"If Herbert did, what's it got to do with you?"

"It isn't fair. Can't you see we've no right to take

136

money you get that way?"

Maimie was furious. To have her kindness and generosity thrown back in her teeth like that. It was insufferable.

"You bloody little fool. You talk as if I earned half-crowns outside Euston Station."

"You don't understand what I mean." Tania struggled desperately for words. "What I mean is, Nannie or Daisy or me, we wouldn't get money your way, we haven't the courage, and we'd be shocked if you asked us to. And the other two would be shocked if they knew about you. Then why should we turn round and let you get money for us in a way we wouldn't get it for ourselves, even if we could? It's not exactly that I think it's wrong what you do. One must have money, I know that. But I should hate it so, having to let them maul me about. Daisy would hate it, Nannie would hate it. Even if you don't hate it we can't let you be mauled about for the lot of us. Oh, Maimie, I know I explain badly, but do try and understand."

"Of course, you're a scream. You make me feel like the bad woman on the films the way you talk. I haven't got a paid job with Herbert, or with anyone else. I don't earn money. It's just that I'm nice to them, and they like to be nice to me."

"I know all that, but I put things so badly. But it doesn't alter the point, we can't take that twenty-five pounds."

"We! I like that! I thought I gave it to Daisy."

"Daisy can't take it."

137

"My God! you are the cat's whiskers. We can't take it! Daisy can't take it! Very well then, how do you propose I get it back? Do you want me to go to them with tears in my eyes, saying: Nannie dear, I didn't come by that money purely? Hand it back. It might sully little Daisy's virginity."

"Don't be furious with me—you must take it back somehow. It won't be difficult. Nannie didn't really believe in that horse—but she was glad you told her a lie she could seem to believe."

Maimie jumped up and put on her outdoor things.

"Well, I shall just go in and take the money. It's lying on the mantelpiece. And you can explain to Daisy that she can't have the clothes, and therefore won't get the job, because you were not only narrow-minded, but bloody interfering!"

She flounced into the sitting-room, snatched up the twenty-five pounds, and before Nannie or Daisy had time to protest, she was down the stairs and had slammed the front door.

"Well!" gasped Nannie. "Of all the mean things. To give the money one minute and take it away the next."

Tania came in.

"It isn't Maimie's fault. I made her. She owed that money to somebody. I told her she ought to pay them first." She told the lie badly. Nannie looked at her nervously.

Daisy burst out crying:

"I do think you are mean, Tania. It was me the money was for. Why should you interfere? You was just jealous. And Nannie and me had just planned that you should have something out of it."

"There, there, my lamb. It is hard." Nannie looked at Tania. "But maybe Tania's right."

"I'm most frightfully sorry, Daisy. But I had— well, anyway, you shall have some clothes somehow. I promise."

She sat on her bed. Easy enough to promise, but where? Nannie came in.

"I'm not asking no questions, dear; there's some things as is best left unasked. But about those clothes. What we goin' to do?"

"I know." Tania jumped up. "Where are those things of Howdy's?"

Rose had left such jewellery as she possessed in Nannie's keeping, saying: "Divide it amongst the children when they are old enough not to lose it. And keep something for yourself.

Nannie considered it a sacred trust. She was most unwilling to touch the things, but Tania persuaded. Finally she fetched the shabby little morocco case. A gold watch. A gold chain. Three rings. Five brooches. Three curb chain bracelets. And some charms.

"There, that's the lot. An' you can't 'ave it till you're grown-up. For so I promised Miss 'oward."

"I don't want to have it," Tania protested. "I only want to borrow."

"Borrow? What d'you mean?"

"Pawn."

Nannie was really shocked. Pawn! Ladies and gentlemen didn't pawn. That was a thing only the roughest of the rough would do.

"I've never seen a pawn ticket, an' I 'opes I never shall."

"Well, you shan't now," said Tania, picking up the case. "And I'll have all these things back long before we're grown up."

She put on her hat and coat. Slipped the case under her arm. And went out.

A pawnshop had three gold balls outside it. Tania knew where there was one. It looked from the outside like a grand jeweller's, but there were the three gold balls. She peered in. There were people buying things at the counter. She was ashamed to go in until they had left. Her heart was beating terribly fast. She couldn't breathe properly. Her knees would shake. She hated hanging about outside like that. She felt all the passers-by must guess what she was going to do.

"This," she thought, "is how murderers feel when they buy the knife to do the deed."

The people came out of the shop. They were talking and laughing.

"It was hardly worth while having the diamonds reset, I wear it so seldom. But I do hate broken things about."

Tania glared after them, envious of their ease. They'd no need to feel ashamed. She threw up her head. Well, now for it.

"I want," she said to the very suave gentleman behind the counter, "to pawn something."

The gentleman, still suave but somehow more familiar, directed her by a gracious swaying movement, half bow, half point, to go into the inner room. In the inner room she found an easier man to deal with. He treated her like an old friend.

"How are we to-day?"

She handed him the morocco case.

"I want to pawn these."

He smiled at her.

"Not very old, are you?"

Terrified, she wondered if there was an age at which one might pawn things—like not being allowed to go on the stage—or go into a public-house. Perhaps one couldn't pawn if one was a child.

"I'm twenty-one, I know I don't look it."

But the man seemed to have lost interest in her age. He was turning over Rose's jewels.

"How much do you want for these?"

Tania was flabbergasted.

"Gracious! I don't know. I thought you'd say what I could have. What I want," she said, confidentially, "is enough for a frock, a coat, a hat, and if possible some shoes. I should say I couldn't do with much less than fifteen pounds."

He laughed, but in the end, after various weighings and scratchings at the things, he gave her fifteen pounds. He didn't want to keep the box or the charms. But she refused to take them.

"I've reasons for preferring it should all be kept together."

"Hope you get some pretty clothes," he called after her.

"Oh," she came back and explained. "They are not

141

for me, they are for my sister. Forgive me," she added, "I'm sure you're always careful, but you will be extra careful of that box?"

He looked after her and laughed.

"Comic little piece," he thought.

Tania, gripping the fifteen pounds carefully, reached the flat. She hurried into her bedroom and locked the door. Daisy was at school, Maimie out doing the shopping. She would be undisturbed. Now where should she hide her pawn-ticket? Her dressing-gown caught her eye. She seized hold of her scissors, and ripped open the hem, popped the pawn-ticket inside it, and carefully sewed it up again. Then she breathed a sigh of relief, no one could find her shameful secret.

It was a very dapper and grown-up Daisy who arrived with Madame at Leon Low's office. Rather longer skirts, a small smart hat, and a well-fitting coat, had aged her wonderfully. She didn't say much, but she met with approval.

"Smart little thing, looks much older than I expected," Leon Low said to Madame. "Bring her along to the audition, and we'll see what George says about her."

George was the great George K. Gene. He was an American, famed for his production of ballets not only in his own country, but all over Europe. Leon Low considered the success of his new revue assured as soon as he got the great man inside the theatre. He was to arrange and produce two ballets. At the audition he sat in the stalls. He was a silent little man, occasionally he muttered, "Oh gee!" Mostly he just sighed.

Daisy was fortunate. If there were one thing George K. Gene did like in his dancers, it was youth. You could not be too young for him. At twenty-five you were definitely too old. He engaged Daisy.

There was a little money left over from the fifteen pounds. They spent it on a grand tea to celebrate the event.

When Daisy's rehearsals started, Tania found it a struggle not to be jealous, or rather not to show how jealous she was. There was she, week after week, creeping round from one dreary music-hall to another. And there was Daisy, with a short ride in the Tube to Piccadilly, pleasant easy rehearsals, exciting fittings for lovely frocks, lots of exquisite photographs taken of her by admiring photographers, and her picture, and little things written about her in almost every paper you picked up. She was so terribly lucky, and she never realised her luck, she'd just been born with a gift, and there it was. She had stepped straight from the academy to a leading part on tour, and a larger salary than her sisters ever earned. She had never been part of a troupe. Never had to be one of Pansy's Peaches.

Maimie got into the chorus of the revue. It was no common chorus. The twenty girls that composed it were supposed to be the loveliest and most gifted in the world. Every girl had been chosen with the utmost care. A very high standard of dancing and some sort of voice were required, apart from an exquisite face, perfect legs, and an exceptional figure. Maimie hardly dared to hope. She wasn't worried about her face, or legs, or figure; obviously they were well above the standard, but was she clever enough? Luckily for her, Madame's training had been thorough. Maimie had been lazy, and she had given up training far too soon, but somehow technique had been drilled into her. And once it was there she couldn't forget it. So she was engaged.

The revue went with a bang. Daisy achieved a mild fame. That is to say, full-page portraits of her appeared in papers such as the *Sketch* and the *Tatler*. All the most intelligent critics gave her good notices, they thought she had a future. Her management kept her age a secret. Thirteen was too young. They let it be understood that she was fifteen, a much more attractive age. She had endless letters from her audience. Tania answered them for her, as with her school-work she had very little time. Nannie would bring the letters home from the theatre, and each morning after breakfast Tania sat down and replied to them. As a rule they only required a signed postcard popped in an envelope. But sometimes when they asked direct questions, she amused herself answering them. Daisy never saw either the original letters she had received, nor the answers. So Tania had a free hand. "Was her hair naturally red?" "Yes," Tania wrote. "All my family have had red hair, in my old family home we are known as The Red Whicharts." Another correspondent asked why she had gone on the stage. Tania amused herself with a reply in which

Daisy said that the stage had never been her choice of a career. "My old father is a Roman Catholic Priest, so old and infirm now that he cannot work. I wished to enter a convent, but I could not only think of myself, so I threw my wishes aside, took to the stage, and became the dancer you see me to-day."

Not long after the revue started, Pansy Daw's suburban tour came to an end. Madame told Tania she was to finish with the Peaches. They were going for a long tour of the northern music-halls. Tania was already too tall, and in any case pantomime was coming on, she ought to be getting something better. Tania was delighted. If Madame thought she was too big for a Peach, that settled it. The mere thought of finishing with the Peaches sent her spirits soaring. There was no money anxiety at the present. Maimie's twenty-five shillings coming in regularly, and Daisy earning a good salary, out of which Nannie was saving enough to redeem Rose's jewellery in the spring, and she herself bound to get some sort of pantomime job. Meanwhile she would have a glorious holiday. Tania set out for the theatre with the lightest heart she had had for weeks. She looked so cheerful that Phoebe, Pansy's very confidential maid and dresser, said:

"Come into a bit, dearie? You looks 'appy tonight, generally you looks like a funeral——"

Tania started, she'd been dreaming.

"I'm going to have a holiday, Phoebe."

"Aren't you comin' up north with us?"

"No, I'm stopping here. I shall go into a pantomime."

"Well, maybe it will suit you better. You've always been on the tall side for us—and a job all dancin' will suit you better, not exactly a singer, are you, dear? Mind you, you've got a nice voice, but you 'aven't got the pep some'ow. Pep counts for more than singin' in our business. Look at Miss Daw, her voice ain't nothin' amazin'—and now look at her."

Tania looked. So that was what they thought of her voice, no pep. It was true, pep was what Pansy possessed. She sighed. Oh well, another dream gone west.

On finishing with the Peaches, she thankfully spent her evenings at home with a book. Daisy pressed her to come to the theatre with her, but Tania said she hated theatres and saw no reason to enter one when she hadn't got to. She would never have gone had not Daisy found out that Miss Poll was the wardrobe-mistress.

Miss Poll was unchanged. Although in such a position of importance—

"Ask me how I got it, dear—I'll tell you I don't know. As I always says—must 'ave been born lucky. It all came of me comin' along to oblige. An' Miss 'erbert, 'er as was in the wardrobe, fell down an' broke 'er leg. So they says to me, 'Carry on till she comes back,' an' that's where I says I'm born lucky, because Miss 'erbert she dies po'r thin'—weak 'eart she 'ad—course I was sorry an' all that—still luck's luck."

"Wish I had luck," sighed Tania.

"Luck don't come by jus' sitting' at home waitin' for it. It wouldn't 'ave come to me if I 'adn't 'ave been in the wardrobe to oblige would it?" They were having a mid-evening cup of tea. Miss Poll drew Tania's cup towards her. She sucked her teeth, then nodded wisely.

"Luck's comin'. I see a long journey by sea an' land. An' see those tea-leaves there—that'll be an important meetin'—maybe with the boy you're goin' to marry. Oh my! an' you're goin' to 'ave some money, I never did see so much money in a cup. I see a gold ring and letters, and a present of money from a dark man." She laid down the cup, and gazed at Tania as if she were seeing her for the first time. "Luck indeed! Me talkin' to you of luck—why, your cup's cram full of it—all you've got to do is to 'elp yourself to it."

"It's easy to talk, but how——?"

" 'eaven 'elps those 'oo 'elps themselves, remember," replied Miss Poll sententiously.

Sitting in the Tube on the way home, Tania thought of her tea-cup—of course it was all rot—but it was true that luck didn't come by sitting about waiting for it. Her luck would come when she learned to drive—to fly—she knew it. Yes, it was time she got herself out of this rut. To-morrow she'd find out about a driving-school, find out how you got a mechanic's certificate. She threw up her head, her eyes shone. Climbing the stairs to the flat, she might have been climbing Olympus. The telephone bell rang.

"Is that you, Tania? It's Muriel speaking. I've been trying to get on to you all the evening. Madame says come round early to-morrow. You are to go to an audition."

CHAPTER 13

The most remarkable thing happened. Daisy's relations found Daisy. Daisy of all people, who was supposed to have no relations, not even one written on the fly-leaf of a Bible.

They turned up after a matinée. Tania and Nannie were having tea with Daisy in her dressing-room. The door-keeper brought up a card. "Mrs. James Higgs," and underneath in pencil, "And Mr. James Higgs."

"Mrs. James Higgs? Now who on earth?" said Daisy.

"Better see 'em, dearie. May have seen you from the front and goin' to make you an offer." Nannie was always hopeful for her darling.

Tania took the card.

"I shouldn't think it's that. Look at the address, 'The Pines,' and in Surbiton."

Mr. and Mrs. Higgs were shown in. Their accent was refined and careful. They looked prosperous. Mrs. Higgs had an expensive fur coat, Mr. Higgs a large diamond pin in his tie. They were awkward and embarrassed. They sat side by side on the very edge of the sofa, Mr. Higgs nervously spinning his hat round on one finger. He stared at Daisy.

"To think as we should have found you here."

"It's often we pictured this meeting," Mrs. Higgs added, "but never like this."

Daisy, completely mystified, simply sat with her

148

mouth open and gaped. But Tania jumped to her feet.

"I know, you are Daisy's illegitimate grandparents from Balham."

"No longer Balham, but Surbiton, dear." Mrs. Higgs was flustered. What a way to put it! "Illegitimate grandparents!" "But you are right, I'm little Daisy's grandmother."

Mr. Higgs stirred himself.

"And I'm the young lady's granddad, and proud to own it."

It seemed that Mr. Higgs had bitterly regretted that he had let the baby leave his house. He had no sooner heard the taxi drive away than he had begun to regret. The house had been cruelly empty without their Daise'. A baby would have cheered things up. They could have moved with her to another part of London. No one need have known what had happened.

"Why didn't you put on detectives to look for her?" asked Tania, interested.

Well, Mr. Higgs had his pride. Detectives were a nosey lot. Their Daise' was dead. Didn't want folks prying round to know why she'd died. But they'd always kept their eyes open. Always hoped.

"Then last Sunday," Mrs. Higgs broke in, "there was a picture in the *Sunday Pictorial.* 'Why!' I said, 'if that isn't the image of our poor Daise'.' Well, we kept looking, and the more we looked the more like we thought it was."

"Then I said," Mr. Higgs added, " 'Mrs. H., if you think it's like our Daise', you shall go and see for

149

yourself. For otherwise it will be fidget, fidget, all the time.' " He turned to Nannie. "You women are all alike."

Nannie, too excited to speak, merely nodded vaguely. Mrs. Higgs took up the story:

"So we came this afternoon, dear, and as soon as you tripped on to the stage with those red curls and blue eyes, I burst into tears. 'Why!' I said, 'it might be our Daise' come alive again.' "

Mr. Higgs drew out an enormous pocket-handkerchief, and blew his nose loudly. Nannie thought there were things she and the Higgs' had better discuss alone. They might not be what they said. They seemed respectable enough, but then you never knew. Dreadful stories of kidnapping she had heard.

"Tania dear, you an' Daisy go outside for a bit."

In the next quarter of an hour the grandparents established their authenticity beyond argument. The baby clothes Daisy had worn. Her weight when she was born. Mrs. Higgs remembered every detail. Nannie in return told them of Daisy's babyhood. Of her sisters. Of her talent for dancing which had led to them all being trained for the stage. Of the death of Rose. Of herself as godmother and guardian.

"If I may say so," said Mr. Higgs when she had finished, "you done very well by her, very well."

The next day Daisy and Nannie lunched at Surbiton. The Higgs' car and chauffeur called for them. They went impressed but nervous. Daisy returned home enchanted. She couldn't stop telling

Tania of the glories of her grandparents' home. Even Maimie stayed to listen.

"Imagine! They've got the loveliest house with the neatest garden. All the flowers in rows—a different colour in each row—and such a pretty drawing-room—everything pink—and heaps of pink bows—and there was a parrot called Cocky, and a lovely little white fluffy dog called Flossie—and it wore a pink bow to match the drawing-room. And there were heaps of pictures all in bright gold frames. And on the landing halfway up the stairs there were lots of ferns—with green bows on them to match the carpet. And the spare bedroom was all blue—and when I go to stay that's where I'm to sleep—and the bed has blue bows on it——"

"Gracious!" Tania interrupted. "How many yards of ribbon do they use?"

But Daisy was far too excited to notice interruptions.

"Some people came to tea—and grandfather said: 'This is my little granddaughter.' Imagine it! It felt like being in a play to hear somebody say that about me."

In their bedroom Maimie said to Tania:

"Her relations sound awful, poor kid. If that's the sort I had, I'm glad I burnt my Bible."

"Yes, they were fairly awful—but I should think it was fun having relations, even Higgs. Somehow I don't believe my grandmother would be like Mrs. Higgs."

"Why don't you find out? You've got your Mother's address."

151

"It wouldn't be fair. You remember what Howdy said——?"

Nannie was delighted with the Higgs', and she was thankful. She wrote and told the news to "Young Mr. Bray." He was thankful too. He came and saw Nannie, and they had a long talk together. He knew that Daisy was doing very well on the stage, but didn't Nannie think it would be wonderful if Mr. and Mrs. Higgs adopted her? Nannie sighed; it would be wonderful, and what was more, it was quite likely that the offer would be made, but there were Maimie and Tania to consider. Daisy was the largest wage-earner, there was the home to keep together. No, adoption was out of the question.

"But what I says is they're there to fall back upon. It's grand to think them 'iggs' is there if Daisy should need 'em."

The Higgs' for their part were delighted with Daisy. She was all a granddaughter should be, simple, affectionate, grateful, admiring. Nannie, too, such a respectable background—"Our little granddaughter and her old nurse." The only flies in their ointment were Maimie and Tania. Nobody in Surbiton had known the older Daisy, they just accepted the fact that Mr. and Mrs. Higgs had possessed a married daughter who had died when the little Daisy was born. But Maimie and Tania complicated things. The sight of the three girls together would ask for explanations. Daisy and Nannie lunched at Surbiton every Sunday, and were often there during the week as well; the Higgs' couldn't help feeling they ought to ask the others. They did at last, only to find there was no need to search for further excuses, for Tania only accepted once, and Maimie never came at all.

"I couldn't live up to the bows, darling," she explained to Daisy. "I'd be afraid of mucking up your chances."

On Tania's one visit she was horribly bored and rather frightened. Daisy sank into the position of "Little Granddaughter" so naturally. The Higgs were obviously delighted with her. Would the day come when they wanted to keep her altogether? Would Daisy cease to be one of the family? Tania had planned a glorious career for her. Grand world tours, vast fortunes, and finally—for that was what Daisy would really like—a wedding, perhaps to a duke or earl. Was it all to end in Surbiton?

The Higgs' gently tried to discourage Daisy from talking of her sisters in front of people. When she was in their house, they would have liked her to use another surname. Whichart! Such a queer name. Sort of name that made people wonder if they'd ever heard it before. With Daisy's history it was so much better that people shouldn't have anything to wonder about. Daisy had explained how they came by it, which made the name seem worse, almost blasphemous. But Daisy, so gentle and amenable in other ways, utterly refused to use any other name, and was quite unquenchable on the subject of her sisters. She admired them enormously, she couldn't believe that her grandparents and their friends weren't interested in such obviously interesting people—in fact many of the people she met at Surbiton were tremendously interested, they liked hearing how Maimie's friend Mr. Rosen had given them all tea at Rumpelmayer's—and how Tania had been one of Pansy's Peaches; in fact they seemed extraordinarily interested in even the smallest detail of their lives.

The Higgs' were distressed, but they couldn't do anything, they could only hope that people weren't talking. They discussed the possibility of asking Daisy to live with them. Of separating her from her unfortunate background. No good while her revue lasted, it was better she should live nearer her work. Theatre hours upset a house so. Besides, there was her school. It all wanted a lot of thinking out. They'd like to do well by her. Like her to have a chance of meeting really nice people. There were lots of nice boys growing up in the neighbourhood. Nice for Daisy to have a chance to meet nice boys. When girls and boys grew up together you never knew— They were sorry she was on the stage. They hadn't liked it for her mother. They thought it was a dangerous profession. And they had been right. Look what it had led to!

Maimie watched Daisy sinking further into the arms of Surbiton with growing satisfaction. Herbert was getting so difficult, insisting on taking a flat. She wasn't sure she wanted him to, he wasn't the only pebble on the beach. Herbert was so silly and jealous. So difficult to manage. Living in his flat wouldn't be all honey. He'd hate to see other boys about the place. Still Herbert was the boy for the money. Didn't mind what he gave you, either, if he could be sure he was the only man you knew. So silly! How could any man be the only man she knew? But if Daisy went to live in Surbiton, well—it would be worth while wangling things a bit with Herbert. Lovely to get away. If Daisy went to live in Surbiton, that would leave only Tania. Tania! There was the trouble. She didn't like to let the kid down. She was so set on keeping the home together, and worked so damn hard for it. Pity she wasn't the sort to like men. Then they could have lived near each other, that would have been grand. She was a little fool to be so stubborn about not using the address in her Bible. No harm in just looking her mother up, just prospecting round a bit to see how the land lay. If she thought she was in the way, if there were a husband and kids and things, she need never use it, she could just come straight back. Still, it was worth having a look round. But Tania was so difficult about things. Still, if Daisy went to live in Surbiton— and—Well surely Tania would see she must do something—couldn't always stay tacked on.

CHAPTER 14

Tania was the only member of the family working in pantomime that Christmas. For the other two, Christmas was only marked by a few extra matinées. This made her dislike her labours even more than usual. The Suburban theatre at which she appeared took the best part of an hour to reach, her performances began earlier than in the West-End; this meant that she started drearily off to work, leaving her sisters seated over the fire, conscious that they needn't stir themselves for another hour at least. She was ballet and chorus this year. She was glad she had stopped being a juvenile, as she went backwards and forwards alone; otherwise it seemed to make very little difference. She was a glorified member of the chorus, as the chief feature of the pantomime, which was 'Aladdin,' was the jewel ballet in the cave scene, with Madame's pupils as various precious stones. Tania was the Ruby. She only appeared for a few moments on her toes, dressed in a tunic of crimson spangles, but the position of solo dancer gave her various privileges. She could never make up her mind whether the slight extra comfort thus earned was worth the discomfort of being made conspicuous.

It was her fifth pantomime, and she was determined it should be her last. The utter futility of the whole business—What was she getting out of it? Not a damn thing. A small salary for a very few weeks at Christmas—most unlikely to earn anything the rest of the year—and yet unless she did something drastic, she would be back at the academy as soon as the pantomime finished, working and training hard—for what? For a chorus job on tour perhaps; if not, for next year's pantomime, and all the time to be bored, bored, bored. Mentally she felt like a sponge. There was just one bright spot. Nannie was handing back to her quite a lot of her salary as pocket-money. It was intended for stockings and gloves; actually it was not spent at all, Tania hoarded it. She kept her savings in an old soap-box, and in bed at night she would take them out, and gloat over her money as though she were a miser. It represented to her freedom; freedom from the boring and cloying life she led at present, because in the soap-box she had the means slowly collecting that would enable her one day to earn money in the way for which she was fitted. She never doubted for one moment that once she had the necessary training she would find the work. She knew with her whole being that she was a born mechanic. In what way she would have a chance to prove this she didn't know, but her prayers always finished: "And oh God, if possible, let me fly."

Towards the end of the run of the pantomime, when her savings amounted to nearly three pounds, she sought expert advice. The stage carpenter had a motor-bicycle, he was always tinkering with it, he knew its inside almost better than its out.

"George," asked Tania, "suppose you wanted to learn everything about car engines, where would you go to learn?"

"I wouldn't want to," said George, meditatively scratching his head, "I knows all I needs to know."

"Yes, I know you do, but suppose you had a taxi, and wanted to be able to repair it?"

"I wouldn't want no taxi, I 'as a fixed job 'ere, taxis is most uncertain."

"Yes, but if it wasn't for you, George, if you knew someone who wanted to learn, where would you advise them to go?"

George gave his head a deeper and more exploratory scratch:

"Well I don't know, I fancy I'd send 'im to a good garridge, nothin' like a good garridge, learn everythin' there——"

A good garage! Now where did one find a place like that? Tania wondered if she knew anybody who would help her. There was Herbert, he always had cars, he must keep them somewhere, but there were objections to asking Herbert's advice. First of all she hardly ever saw him, and never alone, and secondly, if she did succeed in catching him by himself he'd be certain to tell Maimie all about it, and Maimie would tell Nannie and Daisy, and there would be a general fuss. Time enough for a fuss when she had arranged with a garage. No, Herbert would be no good. Then suddenly she thought of the Higgs' chauffeur. She didn't exactly know him, not as a friend; he was just the Higgs' chauffeur, Bristowe, but she had a sort of nodding acquaintance with him, for when he called for Daisy on Sunday mornings, she could never resist wandering out casually to have a look at the car. Of course she had never touched it, she had tried to look as though her looking at it at all was an accident, but in spite of this elaborate pretence, she and Bristowe had decidedly reached the stage of a nod.

The next Sunday morning luck favoured her, for when the car arrived, grey and exquisite, Daisy wasn't ready. And apparently the car, perfect though she looked, and perfectly as she had slid into position at the front door, wasn't at her best. For Tania came down to find the bonnet up, Bristowe's hind portions the only part of him visible, and the car's interior displayed before her admiring eyes.

Bristowe was fond of his car, he treated her as he treated women, and he had a most successful way with women. His method was to humour them; humour them, that is to say, up to a point, the point being the hilt; and then be firm. So with the car. He gave into her in every possible way. She said she wanted more oil when she most certainly did not, he gave her more oil. She said she wanted cleaning when he knew she was already spotless, he gave her another wipe round. But just once in a way he was firm. He would say: "No, my lady, you don't!"—and he was saying: "No, my lady, you don't!" on this particular Sunday morning. She had disgraced him, she had refused to do a simple little hill in top. She who could have climbed Everest in top if she had put her mind to it. He was disgusted with her. A poor way to behave on a Sunday morning.

Tania, unable to resist so entrancing a spectacle,

leaned over Bristowe and stared at the car's vitals. Bristowe unscrewed various bits of her, he waggled bits of her, and the more he unscrewed and waggled, the more entranced Tania became. A feeling of kinship stole over them both, and before they knew where they were, they began to talk. Bristowe told Tania about the car, how he had chosen it for the Higgs' who knew nothing about cars, how she ran just as sweet as sugar as a rule, but how this particular Sunday she wasn't running at all nice, not at all nice she wasn't. Tania asked about her speed, Bristowe looked round to be sure no one was listening, and then confessed that given a clear road she could touch eighty, but they—and here he gave a scornful jerk of the head to depict absent Higgs—they thought they weren't safe at thirty, fair sickening Bristowe found it. He'd been in the Air Force during the war, and knew what speed was, of course he'd only been a mechanic, but he'd kept his eyes open. My! that was the life, all the sky to fly in, no white lines and traffic regulations and speed limits. My! it was a bit of all right up there. Tania's lips parted, her breath came in short gasps. How she agreed with him. How right he was in every word he said. She told him she wanted to find a garage where she could get her mechanic's training. He looked serious, he didn't think it was a job for a girl, didn't think there was anything in it. But if it was learning to drive she wanted, well he'd give her a lesson or two. They heard Daisy and Nannie talking on the stairs. Bristowe said quickly:

"Next Sunday when I'm down fetchin' Miss Daisy,

pop out an' we'll fix a time on the Q.T."

Tania trod on air. She went through agonies before the next Sunday. Would he remember?—oh, would he remember? On the Sunday morning she hung out of the window watching for him. He had barely brought the grey bonnet on a level with the front door, before she had raced out to him. He had not forgotten:

"Could you get out on Tuesday morning?—I'm taking that there dog Flossie to the vet, an' I can leave the dog an' pick you up, an' squeeze in 'alf-an-'our, but you'll 'ave to find your own way back, as I daren't be out longer than that or they'll miss me."

Tuesday morning was cold and grey, but to Tania waiting on the corner for Bristowe to pick her up, it was a day to dream about. She never noticed the cold, she was far too excited. And for her, the grey morning had all the colours of the sunset. As the car drew level with her, she slipped into the front seat, giving Bristowe an almost intoxicated smile.

"Have you a licence?" he asked.

She turned her eyes to him, terrified:

"I can't have one, I'm only sixteen."

It was against his conscience, against his better judgment, but he couldn't see the kid look like that; he ought at once to have refused to give the lesson, but those brown, passionately eager eyes weakened his will power.

"Oh well, may as well be 'ung for a sheep as a lamb, but we'll 'ave to stick to the quiet back streets."

Tania had never guessed that it was possible to feel

such ecstasy as she felt as her hands first touched the steering wheel. She turned crimson, her heart seemed to beat in her throat, her eyes filled with tears. Oh, the smooth lovely feeling of the wheel—the delicious throb of the engine—the sensation of power—the knowledge that in obedience to you, this great powerful thing would move fast—fast till she almost flew.

"Oh, Bristowe, isn't she lovely!"

"Never mind if she is or isn't, you listen to me. Now that there lever moves the gears——"

Bristowe was not given to praising women, he didn't hold with it. In his opinion they thought more than enough of themselves as it was. But he was enormously proud of Tania. At the end of half-a-dozen lessons he would have trusted her with his car anywhere. Of course not having a licence he never let her take it out alone, nor had she driven much in traffic, but he knew what she could do. She seemed to have almost an uncanny understanding where cars were concerned, she made none of the mistakes usual to beginners, never got muddled with her gear-changing, never stalled her engine. He didn't praise her exactly, but there was a change in their relationship; from pupil and teacher, they became two enthusiasts with the same hobby. Tania talked to him about her future. He didn't laugh, or throw cold water on her hopes, but he warned her that he didn't see any great opening for a woman in the motoring line, no chances for a woman in racing or tests. Unless she had some backing, he didn't see what there was for her but a chauffeur's job, and those were hard enough to get even for a man. Still, there was no harm in learning how to do a bit of repairing as a start.

Bristowe had a brother, one Alfy, who had a garage down Richmond way. He approached him on the subject of Tania. Alfy gave it as his considered opinion that it would be a waste of the young lady's time, there was very little work about anyway, and none at all for a girl. Still, if it was a bit of teaching she was wanting, he was willing.

It was arranged that Tania should go to the garage every morning from nine-thirty till twelve-thirty, while her pantomime lasted, and extend the hours after that. Alfy, with a jerk of his thumb at the mixture of oil, dust, and cotton waste on the floor, pointed out that she must wear overalls, and mustn't mind "gettin' her hands in a cruel mess." Tania assured him that she didn't consider that sort of dirt, dirt; then she swung miserably about on one leg, wondering how she could introduce the question of money. There was no really good moment to do it, so in desperation she interrupted a highly technical argument on magnetos with:

"Mr. Alfy, what's it goin' to cost?"

Alfy eyed her severely.

"In my garridge," he said in a slow mournful voice, "there ain't no misters, we're the proliteriot we are, an' I'm just Alfy—an' you'll be just Tania. As for cost, well now——" He scratched his head and looked to Bristowe for assistance.

Bristowe, who knew all about Tania's three

163

pounds, suggested two pounds as a start, and see how they went. Alfy agreed that was the best way, nothing like seeing how you went.

Tania went home on the Underground in a state of enchantment, and it was not till she reached the flat that she remembered that she must tell Nannie what she was going to do, and that Nannie would most certainly disapprove. There was no doubt about it, Nannie would have to be told the truth, it was impossible that she should just slip off every morning and never explain why.

Nannie most definitely disapproved. Tania was a help in the flat—why should she want to go messing about in a dirty garage?—overall or no overall she'd ruin her clothes—and where was the money coming from, with the pantomime coming off?—it was a most ridiculous idea, and Tania ought to be ashamed of herself for even thinking of such a thing.

Maimie and Daisy backed Tania up. Maimie was astounded that anyone would actually pay to do hard work and make her hands a mess, and Daisy could not understand why, when she could stop in a nice clean flat, she should want to spend her time in a dirty garage among a lot of rough men. Still, Tania did want these extraordinary things, and they would not have her trodden on—Maimie said:

"Oh, leave her alone, Nannie, can't she spend her pocket-money how she likes? She's worked hard enough for it, God knows."

"Yes," agreed Daisy, "working in that horrid old pantomime, and you know how she does hate it."

Tania looked at them both, she felt enormously grateful for their support, it was heavenly of them to back her up. She knew that under similar circumstances they would have shown their gratitude by throwing their arms around her neck, telling her she was "a lamb," or "a perfect pet." She couldn't bring herself to do anything like that, but a warm glowing feeling stole through her. Hidden deep inside her was a love for her sisters that amounted almost to worship, but she was never at all sure that they felt the same about her. She tried hard to find words to thank them, but failed; it was so hopeless to thank people who were used to your reticence, and would think you a damn fool if you tried to put your feelings into words.

She was to start work in the garage on the following Monday. For the great day she bought some jeans. She put them away in a drawer, but she couldn't leave them there, she had to keep taking them out and looking at them. Although they had come straight from a shop, they already had a sort of garage smell.

The garage life seemed to Tania as near the life of Heaven as was possible while still on earth. She told her sisters in a burst of enthusiasm that it was like Sussex. They stared at her open-mouthed:

"Why, what do you do?"

"Oh, just learn how to repair the cars, you know."

"You can't call that like Sussex," Maimie gasped. "And look at your hands, they get worse every day, and they were the best part of you."

Tania examined her long, thin, brown hands, they

certainly were ingrained with oil.

"I don't think hands matter much," she observed cheerfully. "Different for you and Daisy, but who looks at mine? and everyone's hands are awful at the garage, you should just see Alfy's."

"Alfy! Will you listen to her?" Maimie groaned. "Before we know where we are, we'll have Tania marrying a man from a garage."

"Well, I might do a damn sight worse," said Tania stoutly.

With the ending of her pantomime she was able to work longer hours in the garage. She took sandwiches with her, and worked till the last possible minute before flying to catch her train for her classes at the academy. With the result that she arrived there in such a state of grease and grime that she was forced to creep in like a criminal, her hands hidden in her gloves, and make a furtive dive for the cloakroom, where she had a hasty wash and brush-up, before facing Madame's exceedingly observant eye.

Now that freedom was almost within sight, she could stomach the academy better than she had done all the years she had been there. It was the end. She was very unlikely to be offered another engagement before next Christmas, and long before that she intended to have a chauffeur's job. She would be old enough for a licence in June. She knew jobs for a woman were hard to find, but she felt it in her bones that she was going to be one of the women who found them. She was so sure that she had finished with the stage for good, that on the last night of the pantomime she nearly gave away her grease-paints to save carrying them home.

Madame had Tania on her mind. She liked the child. She knew she would never be much good, but she was a reliable and a hard worker. Then this term she was not so plain, she had filled out a little and though still painfully thin, was less angular. Madame had often regretted that the child looked so sad, but this term she seemed quite different, she had a light in her eyes, and more personality somehow.

"Must fix Tania, fix Tania, fix Tania," she said to Muriel.

Muriel agreed, but pointed out that it wouldn't be easy. Tania was certainly growing much prettier it was true, but she still hadn't the kind of looks for a West-End chorus, and she completely lacked push, which, when all was said and done, was more important than looks. If there was a back row, Tania always found it. Still, she was a nice kid, and they would try her for the first job going.

Tania was working at the bar. It was an exercise she had done for the last eleven years, so although her feet were performing it adequately, her brain was saying: "Then take out the plug—clean the——"

"Tania dear, you're wanted," Muriel stood beside her.

"Who? What? Oh dear, what for?" Tania returned to the academy with a thud.

"Madame, an audition, she's got a bloke of sorts in there."

"Oh my God, look at my hands, and look at my

romper."

"Well, there's no time to wash or change, so slip along."

Tania slipped. The man in Madame's office wasn't her idea of a manager, he didn't look rich enough somehow; he'd an ordinary blue suit, and he was smoking a cigarette. Pantomime managers smoked cigars.

"Come in, Tania, come in, Tania, come in, Tania. Mr. Ian Long, Mr. Ian Long, Mr. Ian Long."

The man got to his feet and smiled at her. He had, she noticed, rather long black hair, getting up disturbed it, he swept a lock off his face with a gesture. Seeing this, she decided he was a dancer looking for a partner. He took her hand.

"Do you love our Bard?" he asked

Tania nervously scrubbed the toe of her ballet shoe up and down the floor. "Love our Bard," she thought. "Now what the hell's the poor fool talking about?" She saw Madame making nodding signs, so she answered vaguely:

"Yes."

"Nothing like him. Read him, and you've read life." On this profundity, Mr. Long released her hand.

He was certainly loopy, Tania decided.

"Like to see her dance? See her dance? See her dance?"

Tania lit up, here at last was something she understood. But Mr. Long was still behaving queerly. Pantomime auditions had taught her to expect an "I suppose I've got to look at you" attitude to job-hunting dancers. But Mr. Long said:

"If I may, please."

They went into a small empty practice room, an accompanist was rung for. To her horror Tania heard Madame say:

"Classic dance, classic dance, classic dance."

If there was one dance which she loathed more than another it was a dance they had learned for a charity matinée, which was vaguely known as "Classic Dance." It was performed to the music of Mendelssohn's "Spring Song," and it required floating draperies, and a wreath of flowers to hold in your hands. In a rather grubby romper, which was so short that it left exposed every bit that could be decently described as leg, she felt peculiarly hopeless. However, the music started, Madame's eye was on her, gloomily she got up on her points, and meandered across the floor. She was at no time a good dancer, but on this occasion she was at her worst. Worried by the lack of draperies, fussed at having to wave her extremely grimy hands in the place of the wreath of flowers, she gave a deplorable performance. As she finished, she saw Madame's sad eye on her, marvelling that she could teach a child for so long, and it still dance so badly. She glanced in a hang-dog way at Mr. Long. He wouldn't of course engage her after an exhibition like that. But Mr. Long continued to be most peculiar. Seeing the dance was finished, he leapt to his feet, swept back his hair, and hurrying across the room, seized her hand again, but this time he kissed it.

"My dear," he murmured, "I know an artist when I

see one."

Tania's mouth fell open. What the hell was this man anyway? One thing was certain, he couldn't be a dancer, or she would never have got away with a performance like that.

Mr. Long pulled a small red book from his pocket, skimmed through it with practised fingers, found the page he wanted, and handed the book to Tania.

"Would you read this to me?"

She found it was a copy of "A Midsummer Night's Dream," and he was pointing at the part of the fairy. She supposed she must have read it before, they'd done "A Midsummer Night's Dream" at school. She started haltingly:

> "Over hill, over dale,
> Thorough bush, thorough briar,
> Over park, over pale.
> Thorough flood, thorough fire."

She grew more into the swing of the lines. A little warmth crept into her voice:

> "I do wander everywhere,
> Swifter than the moon's sphere;"

"Gracious, that's nice," she thought. "Can't have read it before, or I'd have noticed that——"

> "Farewell, thou lob of spirits; I'll be gone:
> Our Queen and all her elves come here anon."

"That'll do, thank you," said Mr. Long. He spoke in a pleased voice. He turned to Madame:

"A lovely speaking voice, though inexperienced of course. She'll do very well."

Tania gathered from what followed that Mr Long was a Shakespearian actor, that he wanted someone to teach the dances in "A Midsummer Night's Dream," and to play a few tiny parts. He gave her a list, on it was written:

Dream—Fairy.
Julius Cæsar—Lucius.
Henry V—English Herald.
Macbeth—Fleance.

"There'll be some bits and pieces," he said, "but these will do you to be getting on with. I'll explain to Madame Elise about tights and shoes for you. The tour opens three weeks from Monday."

"Tour!" Tania exclaimed. "But I can't possibly go on tour, I thought it was for London."

"Rubbish, rubbish, rubbish, easily arranged, easily arranged, easily arranged," said Madame firmly.

"I expect you haven't been on tour alone before, have you?" asked Mr. Long kindly. "But don't worry, I'll talk to Barbara Dane about you, she's my leading lady, she's a dear, and I'm sure will arrange that you can live with her.

Tania, painfully conscious she was fighting a losing battle, could only repeat breathlessly:

"I can't go on tour, I can't."

"Rubbish, rubbish, rubbish," said Madame, and dismissing her with a nod, picked up the telephone.

Tania stood in the passage feeling desperate. Madame was of course ringing up Nannie. Nannie would be delighted, for she would earn money, and be taken away from the garage. She couldn't bear it. She rushed into the cloakroom, it was empty. She shut herself into a lavatory, and leaning against the door, shook with silent sobs. She cried so seldom that once she had started it was difficult to stop.

"I can't bear it," she whispered. "What's the good of trying—I'll never get away, never, never, never—a tour! just as I've started at the garage—I can't bear it, I can't, I can't."

CHAPTER 15

Tania arrived home to find her family entranced at her good fortune. She accepted the situation. If they thought it luck, they could go on thinking so.

"Fancy," said Daisy, "I never thought any of us would act in a real play. Imagine it! Shakespeare! Aren't you thrilled?"

Tania was made to recount the story of her audition. They were not interested to hear how badly she had danced, but they were spellbound at her description of Ian Long, and of her reading the part of the fairy. Both Maimie and Daisy said they would have died of fright if they had been asked to do it. Tania produced the list of her parts.

"I'll get my Shakespeare," said Daisy. "Then we can see exactly what you've got to do."

They started with Julius Cæsar. Carefully examining the list of characters—

"Seems to come on with the troupe," Maimie observed, "look at them! Varro, Clitus, Claudius, Strato, Lucius, Dardinius. I expect you'll find on the programme, 'Servants to Brutus—Played by Madame Elise's Little Marvels' "

Only Daisy had studied the play at school, and she knew very little about. So it took them some time to find the part.

"Oh gracious! Look!" Daisy pointed to the stage direction—"Music, and a song."

"I shouldn't worry about that," said Maimie consolingly, "I expect they'll cut it, and put in a dance."

They turned to "A Midsummer Night's Dream." None of them had seen it acted, so they found it hard to visualise.

"Seems to be it will be back to good old panto," remarked Maimie. "I expect you'll find Puck comes up through a trap, dressed like the Demon King."

They carefully searched "Macbeth" for Fleance. When at last they found the part, Maimie was sarcastic—

"Well, I'd give it up, you'll never learn a part that long."

"I like that!" said Daisy. "You that's only had to say: 'This way, sir'—to talk like that. I think it's a very nice part."

They lost heart in their hunt through "Henry the Fifth" for the English Herald.

"Well! if he's in it, he's keeping it a dead secret." Maimie shut the book with a yawn.

"Madame says," Nannie broke in, "that there's a very nice young lady, as maybe you could live with on tour."

"Yes," Tania turned a tragic face to her sisters. "Mr. Long said she was his leading lady!"

There was a horrified pause. Their only experience of leading ladies were the various pantomime principal boys, Pansy Daw, and the incredibly grand stars of the revues and musical comedies they had been connected with. Leading ladies, as they knew them, lived in a rarefied atmosphere, of which the outward sign was a plethora of expensive cars, little dogs, scents, and a perfect army of women hangers-on, who ran messages, took down telephone numbers, and generally spread an atmosphere of their star being too wonderful to mix with the humdrum world. Leading ladies on tour, if not quite so grand as the West-End stars, would certainly live up to more or less the same standard. They would live in hotels, or if they chose to live in rooms, would take the whole house. How then was Tania, on three pounds a week, to live with a leading lady? At last Maimie said hopefully:

"I expect she isn't travelling a maid, and wants you to pack for her, and will count that towards paying for your rooms in the hotels." Tania looked so crushed at this suggestion that she added: "Well, don't worry anyhow, she's almost sure to refuse to have you when she sees you."

Tania went to her first rehearsal in a state of jelly. Her teeth chattered, her knees shook, she had difficulty with her breathing. But Mr. Long seemed to notice nothing. He came over to her as she stood quivering in the doorway. Laid his arm across her shoulders, swept his hair back with a grand gesture, and said to his assembled company:

"This is Tania Whichart."

He made this statement with such an air and a flourish, that Tania felt quite embarrassed, and would liked to explain to them all how totally unimportant she was really. But Mr. Long hadn't finished with her. With the manner of one presenting a mother with her first-born, he presented Tania to a tall, dark girl.

"Barbara, here is Tania Whichart. Miss Whichart, this is my leading lady, Barbara Dane."

Tania stared at Barbara Dane in bewilderment. She looked quite poor, she wore no jewellery, and she grinned at her as though she considered her an equal. The most noticeable thing about her was her simplicity. She said:

"You'd better stick to me for the first week or two, and see how we get on. But I expect you'll hate living with me, I'm dirty about the house. Clay, you know."

Tania didn't know. But she was sure she liked Barbara. Leading lady or no leading lady, she didn't believe this one toured cars, and maids, and dogs, and lived in hotels.

The rehearsal started. They were working at "King Henry the Fifth." Tania carefully followed each scene in her book, praying that she wouldn't make too great a fool of herself when her turn came. She had never managed to find the English Herald, and desperately scanned the list of people who had to enter in each scene, terrified he might be amongst them. During the whole morning the only time she was wanted, it came as a complete shock to her. They had started on a scene which stated that those present were The Constable of France, The Lord Rambures, the Duke of Orleans, the Dauphin and Others. "Well, unless I'm 'and Others,' this can't be me," she thought, wriggling comfortably back into her chair. Ian Long called to her.

"You dance here, Miss Whichart."

"Oh, do I!" Tania hastily grabbed her attaché case, pulled out her ballet shoes, and began to put them on. She looked up to find the amazed eyes of most of the cast on her, and Ian Long, not waiting for her, but carrying on with the scene. "These people are damned queer!" she thought. On the stage as she had always known it, you were told to dance, and dance you jolly well did, until you were told to stop. But in this show you were told to dance, but apparently expected to remain in your seat. "What the hell were they playing at anyhow?" She threw a despairing glance at Barbara Dane, who caught the glance, and beckoned to her.

"He means you've got to arrange a dance for this scene," she whispered. "I don't suppose he'll ever want you to do it at rehearsal. It's a sort of wild life in a French camp affair, intended as a fearful contrast to the pure life led in the English camp next door, but as a rule none of the company can dance—and all it looks like is a Christmas party at the Y.W.C.A. Those two danced in the scene last tour, I expect they'll do it again." She pointed to a fat, fair girl, and a thin, nondescript one. She dug a finger into the nondescript:

"What about this dance in the French camp, Beatrice?"

"Oh Lord! have I got to do that again? It was awful last tour, and a rotten change for me back into my boy's dress."

"Well, how about Phyllis?" Barbara looked at the fat, fair girl.

"Look at her! Does she look like a dancer? and she

simply loathes doing it, says it messes her up for Alice, and she looks about as voluptuous as a pea-hen in child-birth. Couldn't she do it alone?" Beatrice nodded at Tania.

"Do you think she could volupt?"

They stared at Tania.

"Ask the Old Man," Barbara advised, glancing at Ian Long. "Anyway, she's a dancer."

"Gracious! a real one? Can you get up on your toes?" Tania nodded. "That settles it," said Beatrice firmly. "If she can really dance, let her." Phyllis and I looked fools enough as it was, but if there's going to be a real dancer hopping about the stage, we're off. There are limits."

At this point in the discussion, Ian Long, running both hands through his hair, came across to Barbara.

"Coming along finely, I think, don't you?"

Barbara, who had not paid the slightest attention to the rehearsal during the whole morning, agreed with fervour.

"Marvellously! Is it lunch?"

It was. Everybody leapt to their feet. So Tania got to hers. They all seemed hurrying off, chattering together. She looked at them, wondering where was the nearest place to buy some lunch, and how long one had to eat it in.

"Come on, child, come with us," called Barbara.

"Yes, come along with us," said the other two girls.

They had a most amusing lunch. Tania had her views on leading ladies completely revised. Barbara

178

not only looked poor, but didn't mind owning she was, and the other two girls didn't seem to think it queer. Tania was bewildered. Surely if she was the leading lady she must make a lot of money?

"I'm for bread-and-cheese and coffee," said Barbara, as they sat down in a small teashop. "I've had a cast made of my dragon, and it's cleaned me out."

Tania gathered from the discussion that followed, that although Barbara tried to make her living as an actress, her heart was in sculpture.

"Never sculpt," she said to Tania. "Clay simply eats money, and landladies hate it."

The mention of landladies turned their minds to the question of rooms. Barbara told Tania that she would write and engage rooms for the first month, and after that if they were still living together, Tania could take on the job.

"She won't live with you for more than a month," observed Phyllis. "When she's had a month of daily fights with the landlady about clay on the carpet, she'll find it less wearing to live alone."

The afternoon rehearsal started badly. Evidently Ian Long's lunch had not been a success. Then they were rehearsing over a vegetarian restaurant, and the room allotted to them for the afternoon had walls of a particularly trying shade of blue, which made the company look yellow, dull, and unpleasant. Also the company themselves, owing to a mixture of lunch and a morning spent in a stuffy room, had an afternoonish feeling, and were inclined to yawn. They were rehearsing some crowd effects; Tania found herself standing in a group with the major portion of the cast, emitting grunts and groans on given cues, while Ian Long dashed on to that portion of the floor they were using as a stage, exclaiming:

"Once more into the breach, dear friends, once more."

He sailed along fairly happily with the speech, until he reached that point where he asked them to imitate the action of a tiger. Here there apparently should have been a few "Aye, ayes," from the company. These were missing. Ian Long paused, he sighed, he ran both hands through his hair, and began again:

"Once more into the breach, dear friends, once more."

This time the "Aye, ayes" were not forgotten, and he swept on with terrific fervour until he reached the point where he had to ask them to stand "Like greyhounds in the slips——" and there they broke down absolutely. Evidently they were not being like greyhounds. Tania had no idea how one expressed being like a greyhound, but it was clear even to her that the concerted wail that had issued from them wasn't like greyhounds at all.

"No! no! no!" shouted Ian Long. "It's all wrong. Breathe! Breathe! You are greyhounds straining to be off."

"Oh mercy!" thought Tania, "how does a greyhound breathe? She hadn't time to wonder long, for they started again:

"Once more into the breach, dear friends, once more."

They were getting on splendidly, "Aye, ayes," and ferocious long-drawn "Ah's" coming slick on every cue. Ian Long was being more fervent than ever. "Oh Lord," prayed Tania silently, "let us get past the greyhounds." They were reaching the greyhounds, they all tried to look as much like dogs straining on a leash as possible—"I see you stand"—they tried to breathe like greyhounds, but all that happened was a snuffling, as of bad colds.

"Now we're for it," whispered a young man who was standing next to Tania. Ian Long stopped, he ran his fingers through his hair and stared at them all:

"Oh God! Oh God!" he appealed. His prayer appeared to remain unanswered, or at least he was dissatisfied with it, for he raced into a corner, knelt down, and with both hands clutching his hair, continued: "Oh God! give me patience with these fools, give me patience with these fools."

None of the company moved, or seemed in the least upset, they were evidently accustomed to scenes of this sort. The unquenchable young man next to Tania whispered:

"Wonderful performance, that."

Then suddenly it seemed that Heaven had heard the prayer, for Ian Long got to his feet, and returning to his company with a cheerful smile remarked that they really must get this right, and off they went again—

"Once more into the breach, dear friends, once more."

"How he must hate having to call us his 'dear

friends,' " thought Tania.

Later in the afternoon they reached her English Herald. It didn't look as though it would be difficult.

K.Hen. "Now, Herald, are the dead numbered?"

Herald. "Here is the number of the slaughter'd French." (Delivers a paper.)

But the part was deceptive.

" 'Here—is—the number of the slaughter'd French.' "

"No dear," said Ian Long kindly. " 'Here is the number of the slaughter'd French,' just like that, no emphasis."

" 'Here is the—number—of the slaughter'd French.' "

Ian Long looked at her. He was still kindly, but it was plain he knew that he was dealing with a fool.

"Oh dear, I'm sorry," said Tania nervously. She took a deep breath—" 'Here is the number of the— slaughter'd French.' "

She was kept at it for quarter of an hour. In that time she had used every combination of emphasis possible on the eight words. Finally Ian Long, with the manner of a judge passing a death sentence, told her he couldn't hold the rehearsal up any longer, she must go and work at the line by herself, and he would take her through it again after rehearsal. She sat down crimson with shame, and found herself next to the chatty young man who had talked to her during the greyhound trouble.

"Poor fool," he said.

"I know I am," agreed Tania ruefully.

"Not you, him."

"Oh, but I was terribly stupid, I just couldn't get it right."

"Well, who cares about the bloomin' French anyway? Especially dead."

"I would like to get it right, though."

"Would you?" The young man sounded surprised. "Well, I'll show you how. You are saying 'Here is the number of the slaughter'd French,' and you keep saying it wrong because it's such a damn silly thing to have to say anyway. But if you say: 'Here's the list of French stiffs,' it won't fuss you, natural thing to say, see? Try saying both lines alternately—soon get it then——"

Tania tried; she muttered both sentences : " 'Here is the number of the slaughter'd French—Here's the list of French stiffs—Here is the—' " He was quite right; after a few attempts, she had mastered the line.

"Oh I say, I've got it now. How nice of you."

"Not at all. Name of Tony. I'm on in this," said the young man, and wandered on to the stage.

Tania hung about after rehearsal, waiting for Ian Long to hear her line. He came over to her with a smile:

"Time to go home. Are you going to like playing for me?"

"Oh awfully," growled Tania nervously. "Shall I say the English Herald now?"

"English Herald? No! why? Coming on very nicely."

Tania went home completely puzzled. They were

queer, these high-brow actors. Make a fuss enough to wake the dead one minute, and then half an hour later tell you—it was coming on nicely. When you danced, you got the steps either right or wrong. Didn't seem to be anything like that about acting; still they were quite nice, all of them. She dismissed them from her mind with a shrug, climbed on to a bus, and lolling back in her seat, thought about the garage.

CHAPTER 16

Tania had a curious feeling that she was going away forever. Everyone she knew seemed to be saying good-bye to her. Madame, Muriel, the girls at the academy, Alfy and Mrs. Alfy, Cook, who got an afternoon off especially to wish her luck, and even Violet, whom they hardly ever saw now that she no longer lived in the house, turned up one evening to wish her success.

Maimie was quite envious.

"I wish I was you, Tania, I wouldn't half mind getting away for a bit, life's fairly lousy here."

Tania looked sympathetic.

"Herbert's being too aggravating," Maimie continued, encouraged to further confidences by Tania's silent sympathy. "Seems to think that knowing him ought to be enough for any girl. Well, I'm not like that, I get tired of one damn man all the time. Gets in a perfect uproar if he thinks you are seeing any other man more than twice a year——"

"And who is it you are seeing?" asked Tania, skipping to the pith of the matter.

After some hesitation, Maimie owned that Herbert was terribly jealous of George, Lord George Ronald, a ghastly attractive man, but it was silly of Herbert to fuss about George who was too heavily married for words, got a wife and kids, and family tree, and moated granges, and a bit of shooting here, and a bit

185

of fishing there—all that sort of thing; and as if that wasn't enough, he must needs have the most terrific sense of duty. All the old-fashioned stuff, love of wife and home, and three cheers for the red, white and blue. All that sob stuff.

"Why are you wasting your time on him, then?"

Maimie looked as near embarrassment as she ever looked.

"Don't know, must be a bit stuck on him, I suppose. There's no doubt the man's lousy with attraction."

Tania, busy with rehearsals, and depressed and bored at the thought of the tour, had not been paying much attention to Maimie. But now that she considered her, she realised that she had changed. She who was usually so calm and unmoved had a restless manner. Tania couldn't place it exactly, but she looked as though there was something on her mind which she would like to confide in someone. If it was about being in love, Tania earnestly hoped she would keep it to herself, those sort of things she found terribly embarrassing. She looked at Maimie again; something was wrong, she was sure of it, she must say a word or two to show she was sympathetic.

"Not going to have a baby, are you?"

Maimie looked at her sister with scorn.

"You poor mutt! Haven't I just been telling you that there was nothing doing, and you surely don't think I'm such an idiot as to get careless with Herbert?"

"I think it would be a good plan if you married

Herbert, he's got plenty of money, and he's awfully fond of you."

"Well, I'm not going to—A—because I'd be bored to death, and—B—because he's married already."

"Herbert is! Whoever to?"

"I don't really know, he doesn't like it talked about, they haven't lived together for donkey's years. She's a Roman Catholic and thinks divorce is wrong. I'm damned glad she does, I've enough bother with Herbert as it is, without his being free to marry me."

Tania was sure she ought to say something more, ought to encourage Maimie's confidences. After a pause she ventured:

"This Lord George, I suppose he's so full of the domestic hearth business you don't see him often?"

"Well, I wouldn't say that." Maimie paused—"The trouble is, it's all such a waste of time. I get him worked up a bit, and then the next time we meet I have to start all over again, because in the meantime he's been wallowing in simply abject remorse about what he did the time before."

"If you ask me," said Tania boldly, "I'd leave him alone. You've got such a lot of men in love with you, what do you want him for, with his wife and children and remorse. Is it because he's a lord?"

"Of course it isn't. Oh shut up! What can you understand about it, anyway?" Maimie got to her feet. "You can't tell me anything I haven't told myself. I say to myself every day—Give him up—don't see him any more—what's the good of worrying out your guts about the man?—And then directly I do see him, I get all feeble. Come on, it's no good jawing about it. It's a good world if you don't weaken."

On the Saturday before Tania left, Daisy had planned a farewell tea-party for her in her dressing-room, to which Miss Poll was to be invited. This scheme was frustrated, because Daisy was asked to go on after her matinée, and dance at a big charity fête and bazaar, in the place of some star who was ill. Nannie insisted that Tania should come too:

"It's your last afternoon, dear, an' we'll 'ave tea there, nice 'ome-made cakes they often 'as at these affairs."

Secretly disgusted with the entertainment offered, Tania nevertheless agreed to go. She was dreading the morrow with its coming separations. Even a dreary fête with Nannie and Daisy was better than a flat without them. She had a gnawing pain deep inside her, caused by a suspicion that her departure on a long tour didn't so terribly matter to the others. They would miss her of course, but they were so much less dependent on people than she was. She realised it was stupid to be dependent on people, they would always hurt you, and go on hurting you till you were dead. But there it was, people loving you, and better still, needing you, that was everything in life. That, and doing the work you liked.

The fête was an exceedingly fashionable affair. Tania, in her plain rather shabby clothes, felt out of place, so she went to the dressing-room and sat with Daisy, while Nannie dressed her. But as always when she had nothing to do, she grew cross and restless, until Nannie was exasperated.

"Oh, go an' 'ave a look round the fête, do—gives me an' Daisy fidgets to see you fussin' around like that."

Tania wandered out into the hall. She wandered past an ornate stall devoted to lavender bags, and nightdress-cases, which had six chinless, rather stupid-looking girls, dressed in lavender-coloured crinolines in attendance. And past another stall marked Household, which was packed with opulent rubbish for the home, with exact replicas of the girls at the lavender stall in charge, only these wore green. She stared vaguely at many other stalls, all brightly decorated, all most expensive, and all looked after by women in crinolines. "Gracious!" she thought, irritated, "all these women look most awful fools." She studied them, and tried to find out what it was that annoyed her. "I believe," she decided to herself, "it's because, in spite of the fact that they look most terribly stupid, they seem infuriatingly pleased with themselves."

At the far end of the hall was a tent. For lack of anything better to do she wandered into it. Inside, on a small platform, stood a car. It was not a new car, but it was only about a year old, and had been beautifully repainted. What could a car be doing here? She stared at it enchanted.

"Will you take a ticket for the 'bus? Only ten bob."

It was a cheerful red-faced young man speaking. He'd a book of tickets in his hand. He was so much the most pleasant person Tania had seen during the afternoon, that she hated refusing to buy from him:

"A ticket for what?" she asked.

"A ten-bob raffle for the car."

"Do you mean to say that someone's going to get that heavenly car for ten shillings?"

The young man lit up at once.

"Isn't she a topper? She's mine, at least she was mine. Only I'm going to Kenya on Monday, so my Mother, who runs this show"—he waved an airy hand towards the whole bazaar—"knowing I was going to sell the little bus before I sailed, said she'd hand over a stout cheque for her, if I'd raffle her at this do. So here we are. Why don't you have a dash for her?"

"Good gracious! Me!" exclaimed Tania in surprise. "You surely don't think I've got ten bob!"

"Well, I don't know why not. It's not such a hell of a lot to ask for the tickets," objected the young man. "And, anyway, people who come to these shows are generally rolling."

"But I've not come to this show—at least not to buy—not like that I mean——"

"Well, what have you come for then?"

Tania nodded her head towards the distant Daisy:

"I've a sister here, she's going to dance."

This apparently harmless statement seemed to stupefy the young man. He said nothing, but stared at Tania, till at last she said:

"Well, good-bye. I am sorry I couldn't buy a ticket."

Her showing signs of departure brought the young man back to life.

"I say," he gasped, "you aren't Daisy Whichart's sister, are you?"

"That's right," Tania agreed. "Well, good-bye."

"I say!" The young man ran after her, he stammered a little in his excitement. "I say, I suppose you will think this the most awful cheek, but would you—would you———?"

"Would I what?" asked Tania, to help him.

"Well. Oh I know you'll think it the most awful cheek, but well—you want a ticket for the raffle, and I want———Well, would you introduce me to your sister in exchange for a raffle ticket?"

Tania wrestled with her conscience. Of course the man must be mad, she would never look herself in the face again if she did a thing like that—still, a chance to win a car! But no:

"I couldn't," she said.

"I was afraid you'd say no," agreed the young man, completely crushed.

"You see," Tania explained, "I couldn't be as mean a dog as that. I know Daisy, and I know meeting her simply isn't worth ten bob."

"You mean———?" the young man began to laugh.

"Well, I've done some mean things in my life, but I simply couldn't sell you a pup like that."

The young man went on laughing:

"You are a howl," he said. "What name shall I put on your ticket?"

Daisy was still dancing when they arrived. She was spinning round on her pink toes, her red curls flying, her white skirts billowing—"Phew!" whistled the young man. Tania, rapturously clutching her ticket, whispered to him:

"It isn't too late, think it over. Ten bob's ten bob."

But he didn't hear her, he was engrossed with the dancer. When Daisy came off the stage, flushed with her efforts, and clasping an enormous bouquet, Tania slipped up to her:

"I say, there's an awfully nice man here who wants to know you."

"Who is he?"

"I don't know, but he's awfully nice. Imagine it! he gave me a ten-bob raffle ticket in exchange for being introduced to you. I told him it wasn't worth it, but he seemed to think it was———"

"You didn't tell him I was only fourteen, did you?"

"Of course not, I never told him anything about you, except that knowing you wasn't worth ten bob."

"And he still thought it was?" Daisy was enormously flattered.

Tania made the necessary introduction—she merely said:

"This is him," and hurried off. She looked over her shoulder to see how they were getting on. He looked very happy, she was glad to see, not a bit as if he was regretting his ten shillings. Nannie hurried after her, and Tania suddenly remembered that she had no name for the young man. Nannie vaguely distrusted the entire the male sex—but a young man without a name!———

" 'oo's the young gentleman talkin' to Daisy?"

"Well, Nannie." Tania paused, and fidgeted. "He's

192

the son of the woman who's running this show———"

"Oh! An' 'is Mother sent 'im to thank Daisy for 'er dancin'?"

"Well—I think he's telling her how much he enjoyed it."

"Tania, you look at me! 'oo is the young man? Come on now!"

"It's quite true, Nannie. His mother is running the show, but I don't know his name because I only met him over a raffle ticket."

"An' you stands there, Tania Whichart, an' tells me that you h'introduced that h'innocent lamb to a man as you knows nothin' about?"

Tania pointed to Daisy:

"I don't believe he's doing her any harm. Look at them."

Nannie looked. She sniffed.

"That's as may be. Time will show. Many a young gentleman behaves decent at the start."

"But gracious! Nannie, you talk as if Daisy were a grown-up person. He can see she's a kid, and anyway he's going to Kenya on Monday."

"Kenya?"

"Umm, Africa, not the Egypt end, I think it's somewhere in that bit at the bottom."

"Africa! On Monday?" Nannie sighed with relief. "Well, he can't go too far or too fast for me, and I'll thank you to keep any other young men you picks up to yourself. You've no more sense sometimes than a baby." Clucking and fussing like an indignant hen, she went over to Daisy and told her she must change, it was time to go.

Tania grinned. "Poor Nannie," she thought. "Scared stiff of having another Maimie in the home." Then she giggled. "Gracious! I must be unattractive. Nobody ever bothers who I know."

"I say, thanks awfully." The young man stood in front of her, holding two enormous boxes of chocolates. "I've just bought these. Would you keep one, and give the other to your sister from me?"

He went back to his car. Tania looked after him, then she looked at the chocolates. "Gracious!" she thought, "Daisy's stock is going up."

Early though she had to start for Waterloo the next morning, Nannie, Daisy, and to her immense surprise Maimie, came to see her off. After one look at the company Maimie told Tania she took back every word she had said about envying her for going on tour, never before had she seen such a dreary collection of long-haired, seedy-looking men:

"My God!" she said. "If they ever do take you out, they'll offer you a glass of Horlick's."

However, she changed her tune when Ian Long arrived. It might be a cold Sunday morning, and Waterloo Station, but he triumphed over these slight obstacles, and made a thoroughly impressive entrance on to the platform, with his chauffeur, his secretary, and his man, fussing round him; and knots of passengers and porters recognising him, and whispering the exciting intelligence to each other. His hair was a little wild, and his manner exalted, as though the station, the confusion, and the bustle in no way reached his mind, for his soul had soared to heights where mundane things are not. It was all a pose of course, and Maimie appreciated it as such, but it was enormously effective, and it hid the fact even from her, that here was a lonely, dissatisfied, commonplace man.

Only a few years back, and he had been quite a figure on the West-End stage. The slump in the theatre world, together with the fact that newer and younger men were playing the romantic youths at which he had excelled, had driven him into the provinces. He did very well. He still retained the rather too good looks, which endeared him to his feminine public, and still had the manner of the popular idol. He never admitted that he had retired to the provinces for good, and indeed, given the right play, was still capable of drawing an audience, as his occasional dashes back to the West-End proved. He was a glorious joke to his company, for apart from his poses, never was a man more wife-ridden. She had been Phoebe Pleasant, a very indifferent small-part actress, whom he had met in a touring company in his salad days. Though an indifferent actress, Phoebe was far from being an indifferent business woman. She knew a good deal when she saw one. Ian was a good deal. With those looks, and that acting ability, he could hardly fail to succeed, especially if he had a wife behind him with a little money, who could push. Phoebe had a little private money, and large quantities of push. She was determined to get Ian, she studied him from every angle. Fate played into her hands. One day as she was passing his dressing-room door, he called out to know if she had an aspirin. She had, and while giving it to him she asked if he had a headache. No, he hadn't, but he ran an anxious hand up and down his throat, and over his glands. He thought there was a slight stiffness, he wasn't sure that he wasn't sickening for a cold. He spoke of this possibility so nervously, there was such a strained look in his eyes, that in a flash she learned something which in the ordinary way it might have taken years to discover. He was nervous about himself, a hypochondriac in the making. That did it, she pandered to his failing, made him frightened about himself, and then consoled him with remedies. His friends, who were not on the whole drawn to Phoebe, tried to save him from her, but it was no use; by the time the tour finished he had got used to confiding her every symptom into her receptive ear, he felt it was most unlikely that he would ever find another woman to take such an interest, and worry over him in the way she did, so he married her to keep her on the spot. From that moment he led a dog's life. Realising the enormous sex-appeal he possessed for the females in his audience, Phoebe convinced herself that, given a chance, here was a Don Juan. He was nothing of the sort, for he was far too careful of his health for excesses of any kind, but she couldn't bring herself to believe this, she couldn't prevent women falling in love with him, but she could prevent him from having a chance to return it. "Watch him," she said to herself, "Never leave him alone," and on that

196

principle she built their life together. She was always at his side, save during the few months before her two children were born, and then she saw to it that he was always at hers. She would never have had the children with all the expense and anxiety they caused, had it not been that they were such good publicity. She had them christened Viola and Sebastian, and apart from their admirable photographic qualities, as they grew older, she found them useful. She kept them in a flat in London, in the care of a governess, where they were supposed to work hard at their lessons until she telegraphed for them. Then their lives changed entirely, and they found themselves hurriedly packed and moved to some provincial town, which meant that mother had to be in London, so they had been sent for to—Take care of poor Daddy——. This was fun, but what wasn't fun was the fuss when mother came back. To begin with, her return meant that their holiday was over, and then there was all that awful questioning to be got through. Questionings as to what they had done with every minute while she had been away, and, much more difficult to remember, what daddy had done, and of course not remembering, and getting more tongue-tied and nervous every minute.

On this Sunday morning, Ian had escaped from both wife and children, and had a few unaccustomed minutes of freedom. He spoke to various members of his company, then seeing Tania came over to her. She, covered in confusion, and convinced that every eye on the platform was turned on her, hurriedly, and in a shamefaced manner, introduced her family. He had seen Daisy dance, he congratulated her. This gave Maimie a good chance to study his profile. She decided that if on the old side, he was still desperately attractive. When he turned to speak to her, she looked up into his eyes, and smiled. Phoebe, hurrying late and cross down the platform, saw the group, and in one glance took stock of Maimie——

"Ian, you are tiresome. What are you doing this end of the platform? You knew I should be late, you might have seen that our carriage was all right."

They hurried away to their first-class carriage at the other end of the train, Ian nervously and humbly explaining that his man was looking after it.

Maimie looked at Phoebe's indignant back.

"My God! What was that?"

"Mrs. Long," explained Tania, who had seen the Lady in the distance when she had fetched her husband from rehearsals.

"Oh Tania!" Maimie exclaimed. "I take it all back. I wish to God I was coming on tour with you. The other men may be poops, but Ian's all right. As for that cow of a wife of his—I'd teach her—I'd have him off her."

As the train left the station, the last person Tania saw was Maimie, glaring after the fast vanishing Phoebe.

CHAPTER 17

Tania discovered that touring with Ian Long's Shakespearean Company was infinitely more pleasant than touring with a Musical Comedy. The life was too full and varied to admit of the unutterable boredom which had practically extinguished her on her other tour. And the professional rooms, though as repulsive as ever, coloured by Barbara's wit became objects of amusement.

To Barbara almost everything was amusing, and most things interesting. She lived so completely within herself, that she regarded the outside world and its doings with perfect tolerance. Rather as though she were examining the habits and customs of a country she was never likely to visit. She was amazed at the depths of despair into which Tania could be thrown by uncongenial surroundings.

"Can't you see," she would protest, "how little all this matters? What if the landlady is dirty and has a sniff? What does it matter if you are staying in a back street in Manchester, or Leeds, or Wigan? It may be unpleasant, but it can't touch the real you, the private, utter you that lives in here." She would lay her two hands convulsively on her breast, as though defying Tania or anyone else to see into her Holy of Holies. "If only you'll see life that way, none of this will mean more to you than things seen out of a window."

Tania struggled. But she was incapable of looking

at life quite like that. But the mere fact of having Barbara about the place helped her to laugh at many things, which before she had found merely sordid. She grew really fond of the girl, in as far as it was possible to be attached to someone about whom you knew so little. For Barbara was one of those people with whom, however long you knew them, it was impossible to feel really intimate. Automatically Tania learned something of her mind, for Barbara could no more help shedding ideas than a tree its fruit. When not engrossed in learning a part, she was moulding her clay, and the action of digging into the clay seemed to urge her to similar action on her mind. While her fingers dug into the clay, she dug into her brain. A casual remark that the teapot leaked, or a more involved statement about a twist in someone's character; off she would go. A dozen ideas would slip from her, grown from the seed of a leaking teapot, or a warped character. So many ideas, and all so elusive, that Tania, sort as she might, never picked up one clue that could lead her to say, "This is Barbara!"

Barbara in her own way was fond of Tania. A fact which Tania never grasped, and which would have astonished her if she had. There Barbara would sit with her clay; modelling Tania, on her toes, her head raised, her arms raised, her whole attitude expressing upward flight. As she worked, she dissected her sitter. Tania seemed to her such a jumbled person. To have such a real love of machinery, that the commonest engine was an object of beauty. To want so passionately to master machinery until it served you to its utmost limits, and yet to be yourself so tied to people. To have the brain and spirit that should make a pioneer, anchored to such a hyper-sensitive soul.

Tania altered on the tour. She expanded and throve in an atmosphere of admiration. For to the Shakespeareans who were incapable of the mildest jig, Tania's dancing amounted to genius. She, who had always been the unsuccessful member of her family, found this attitude heaven. She realised that she was not a good dancer, and nothing would ever make her so, even supposing she had the wish. But in her present *milieu* she was not only the best at her particular art among the people with whom she was thrown, but she was its only exponent. This gave her a position which she was quick to feel, and which had a decidedly tonic effect on her, after years of being utterly unimportant, in a world in which the majority of her fellow-workers excelled her. Had it not been that she felt the tour to be a shocking waste of time, she would have been comparatively happy. She got on well with everyone, as the youngest she was treated rather as a pet. But she was incapable of complete happiness away from her sisters. She worried about them. She was never able to forget that it was while she was away before, that they had operated on Rose, and she had known nothing about it. What might not be happening at home now? The letters she received were small comfort. Daisy's were full of the Higgs', never a pleasant subject to Tania. And Maimie's, when she wrote, which was seldom, said so little of her doings that the very gaps made for nervousness.

One afternoon, over their high tea, Tania, driven by acute anxiety, confided her worries to Barbara. Barbara had a copy of "Macbeth" propped up against one side of the teapot, and the little model of Tania leaning against it on the other. In a desultory way she was reading through the part of Lady Macbeth before that evening's performance, but the larger portion of her attention was devoted to the clay figure, whose drying she was attempting to expedite with the aid of the hot teapot. There was only one way to distract her from these occupations, and that was to demand some more tea, which would automatically upset both—

"I do wish I'd get a letter from home," she said, accepting her refilled cup. She dropped the remark casually, but Barbara, who early in their acquaintance had grasped Tania's lack of words, translated her remark into—"It's a week since I heard—please say something to make me see I'm a fool to worry."

"You'll probably hear to-night," she comforted, "but if you don't, I should think of a plausible excuse, and ring them up. It won't cost such an awful lot, and it's worth something not to feel fussed." She prodded the clay to see how it was drying, and catching sight of her copy of "Macbeth," propped it up again against the teapot. "Fussing is a most remarkable time-waster," she went on. "Luckily it's a thing people have to do by themselves, because the moment they fuss in the open, somebody's sure to say—'Why not do so-and-so?'—or, 'Try so-and-so'—and then the fuss is over. But millions of people spend all their lives fussing. Fussing that they've got cancer, when perhaps

202

one visit to the doctor would prove that they've not. Fussing in case something should happen to the people they love, fussing lest they should die, when, for all they know, they themselves may be going to die first." Her voice tailed away, and she returned to Lady Macbeth and her clay. There was a knock on the front door. The landlady showed in Beatrice and Phyllis.

"We've no tea to offer you," Barbara greeted them. "We had a haddock, but we've eaten it."

"We've been to the pictures," explained Phyllis. "So as we had to pass the theatre, we called in for the afternoon post, there was nothing for either of us, but one for you, Tania."

"There you are, Tania," Barbara said with a grin. But the envelope in Tania's hand was not addressed by either of her sisters, it was typewritten. She opened it. "Oh!" she gasped. She swayed forward, and gripped the table. The three girls gathered round her in concern.

"What is it, old thing?"

"Not bad news?"

"Sit down, and tell us what's happened."

"It's not bad news. I've won a car in a raffle."

The story of Tania's reception of good news was one of the Company's stock jokes for weeks. Every member of the Company, with the exceptions of Barbara and Tony, advised her to sell the car. Barbara, who had recognised the gleam in Tania's eyes since she had received her news, for the ecstasy that it was, hadn't the heart to recommend so practical a course. While Tony felt that selling it was simply not to be considered. Obviously everyone was simply crazy to own a car. Why then part with it as soon as you got one? To Tania there was no question of selling. It was the most "Sussexly" thing that had ever happened. The world looked quite different. She woke up each morning with a curious lightness of heart, such as she had never felt before, even as a small child. She knew what she would do. She would run it as a taxi. Long runs, taking about Americans in the summer, that sort of thing. It wouldn't bring in a tremendous amount of money, but it would pay her share in their home, and perhaps help towards keeping the others when they were out of work. In any case she'd be useful to them, for when she hadn't a job on, she could drive them about. Maimie would like that, it might make her more keen on living at home. Daisy might find it handy too, and she wouldn't always have to depend on those Higgs' to drive her everywhere.

She wrote to Richmond. She sent her raffle ticket to Alfy, and asked him to collect the car and garage it for her, and would he let her know what it would cost? Alfy replied with a most businesslike letter stating:

"Yours to hand of the 16th inst.," and it went on to say that he "had the favour of her esteemed order." That he would fetch the car as requested and would garage same. He finished up by saying that terms could be discussed on her return to London, when he had a business proposition to put before her. He signed himself, "Yours faithfully, Albert Bristowe." The only bit of the letter which sounded like the Alfy

Tania knew was a pencilled postscript—"Me and the missus is very pleased at your good luck."

Tania did not write her news to her family. They would not only want her to sell her car, but would want to sell it for her while she was away. They would see no possible point in her paying to garage it during all the weeks she would be on tour, and the thought of her keeping it for good, and trying to make a living out of it, wouldn't enter their heads. She felt mean not to tell them, for that week both Maimie and Daisy wrote rather despondent letters. Their revue was coming off, and the outlook was none too bright. Daisy had been offered a few weeks on the halls, but Maimie hadn't heard of anything. She said in her letter that "things" were being difficult. She thought she needed a holiday, she hadn't been away since Sussex. Perhaps if she went away it would bring everybody to their senses. She thought she might go to Brighton, she knew two nice men there with decent cars. But instead she might come and join Tania for two weeks; she wasn't sure. She would let Tania know later.

In the ordinary way Tania would have been delighted at the thought of having Maimie with her. But now she wasn't sure. She remembered the way Maimie had looked at Ian, and still better the way Phoebe had looked at Maimie. After all, Maimie would only stay for two weeks, so she wouldn't care what damage she did, she'd think it fun. But Tania would have to live out several months' more tour. Months during which she would most probably be in black disgrace, living down Maimie's sins. When, however, a month later she received a postcard from Maimie merely telling her to expect her the week after next, pleasure predominated over any other emotion. The other girls were enormously amused at her anxiety for her sister's comfort.

"My sisters could sleep on the floor for all I'd worry," said Phyllis.

"You don't know Maimie," Tania explained. "She won't stay if she's uncomfortable."

"Then if she was my sister, she could go," Phyllis retorted. "Rooms have been good enough for you for a good many weeks, surely it won't kill your sister to live in them for two?"

"You'll understand when you've seen Maimie——"

"From what you've told me of her, and from the glimpse I had of her at the station, I think you've got that sister of yours all wrong," said Barbara. "I bet you'll find the rooms won't worry her at all."

"I hope so."

But Tania was worried. She remembered her own immediate reaction to depressing rooms. Maimie had never been on tour, didn't know what it was like. Would she take one look at the rooms, and go home?

Maimie turned up, and Barbara's prognostications proved correct. The unattractive rooms meant nothing in Maimie's life, what did matter to her were the amusements offered. Boredom was about the only thing of which she was really afraid.

She was very popular with the Company. Not only with the men, but with the girls. She was always an amusing companion, and they found her clear-sightedness stimulating. Barbara told Tania that she had never met anybody with so few illusions.

"She sees herself exactly as she is, no better, and no worse. She never throws sops to her conscience. I like her."

Phyllis liked her too, for she recognised in Maimie a ruthlessness that she would have gladly have acquired herself. Maimie mixed the ingredients that made up her life, deliberately. She wanted money. She wanted men. As far as the money was concerned, she would have preferred to have inherited it. But she hadn't. Heaven hadn't given her much of a deal. No background, no money. But it had given her a face. A face and a figure which, if made the most of, would provide all she needed. Why then fight against it? It was obviously what was intended?

"I wish I was like you," Phyllis once said to her wistfully. "I wish I wasn't so bloody respectable. Look at me! Poking around in a Shakespearean Company for five pounds a week. I couldn't have as good a time as you do of course, I haven't your looks. But I could have a better time than I do. I think my upbringing's cramped me. Father was a doctor. There was never a lot of money, but always enough. Then he died, and all the money there is belongs to mother. It's a funny thing how much our parents must have changed from the days of their parents. The generation that were parents to our fathers and mothers would never have dreamed of leaving their daughters unprovided for. I had the glorious illusion that so it would be with me. At least a life insurance, or something to keep one from actual want. I never thought one could just be left penniless. But I was. I am."

"But what about your family?" asked Maimie. "I thought that was the only point of a family, that they looked after you. Haven't you any?"

"Dozens of all kinds. But first of all they're nearly all poor. And secondly they put their heads in the sand like ostriches. They hope by not looking they won't see me starve. They know I have months and months out of work, but do they ask me how I manage? Not they! They'd be afraid. I might say I was hungry, and then they'd have to help. Or if I was looking happy and well-dressed, they'd be more afraid still. They'd be terrified what I might say."

"And what would you say?"

"I should love to say—'Isn't it nice? Such a nice man is looking after me. Aren't you all glad to think that, for a time at any rate, I'm spared the everlasting nagging anxiety of having no money?' That's what I should like to say, and in honesty there isn't a retort they could make. But it wouldn't be true. I'm drearily, dully respectable, hoping that a nice man will marry me, and when I'm out of work living honestly, if thinly, by the sweat of my brow, here a day's filming, and there a day's charring. Pathetic story, isn't it?"

"People like you never get what you want," said Maimie thoughtfully. "You think such a lot before you do anything, that nothing ever happens. I never think. I don't sit down and say to myself, 'If I fall in love with so-and-so, will he give me money?' But I just fall in love, and he does, and that's that. You make such a song and dance about everything. So does Tania. You both make me feel like a half-crown tart."

In the middle of the first week of Maimie's visit, Barbara and Tania gave a small tea-party to introduce her to the Company. The talk turned to the inexhaustible subject of the Longs. The latest stories of Phoebe. The Company to a man taking up the cudgels for Ian.

"We shall be without our Phoebe next week," Tony told them during tea.

They were interested at once.

"Why?"

"How did you find out?"

"Who told you?"

"Shh! don't all talk at once, and the 'copper's nark', will tell you where he got his information."

"Go on, Tony. Don't keep us in suspense."

"Well, it was from Brown. Brown," he added, turning to Maimie, "is Ian's valet, dresser, spy, and guardian angel. Up till last night I thought him impregnable. I tried him with tips, I tried him with drinks, but it was no good. He accepted the tips, he accepted the drinks, but he remained the utterly discreet servant. 'This isn't normal,' I thought. 'The fellow must have a tongue somewhere. There must be something or somebody that makes him chat. He can't go through life saying nothing but the dreadful royal "We."—"We were very pleased with the house to-night"—"We were not at our best to-night, we have a slight cold———" ' Never a word about how Brown's feeling, or what Brown thinks. I couldn't bear it. 'I won't rest,' I thought, ''till I've excavated Brown.' And I've done it—I've found the real man—I've discovered his leitmotif. And how do you think I did it?"

An amused chorus of "Hows?" greeted him.

"White port," said Tony seriously. "I never saw anyone have so little power of resistance, or get drunk so quickly, as Brown before a bottle of white port. It's a gift! Brown, who I'd given up offering drinks to, because I thought it was a waste of time. Waste of time, ye gods! If only I'd thought of white port before. For when he was drunk, stupid maudlin drunk, I discovered the big noise in Brown's life, the power that makes his wheels go round. It's hate!"

"Hate! Hate of whom?"

"Our Phoebe."

Laughter greeted this.

"Rubbish!"

"He dotes on the entire Long family."

"Oh no, he doesn't. You should hear him when he's full of white port. I've a pretty healthy flow of language myself, but my little flow is as the bath-tap to the Victoria Falls when it comes up against Brown's."

"But what's she done to him?" asked Barbara.

"If a drunk Brown is to be believed, it's a case of what hasn't she done? Apart from ruining Ian's life, and treating Brown as scum, it seems she's a kind of Lady Macbeth-cum-Vampire-cum-Gorgon. The kind of woman you read about in thrillers, 'a sinister influence dominating hundreds of people'. She 'fair gives Brown the 'orrors.' If he'd lived a hundred and fifty years ago,

210

he'd have crossed his fingers every time he saw her. He said, 'Oh, Mr. Brine—hiccup—she's an 'orror, that woman—a perfec' 'orror—hiccup—fair gives me the sick—thank Gawd she's takin' of 'erself off for a few days next week—hiccup.'"

Maimie had not seen Ian since her arrival. She had been in the theatre one night to see "A Midsummer Night's Dream," but had been hideously bored, and taken herself off to a cinema the next evening. But the conversation entertained her—gave her an idea. What fun to lead Ian up the garden path, and make that cow furiously jealous. The party had broken up, there were only the four girls and Tony left.

"I think I'll come behind with you to-night, girls," she said casually.

Tania looked anxious.

"Why? There are heaps more cinemas in the town; you'll be awfully bored."

"Oh no, I won't, I'd like to come."

Barbara looked at her.

"If all this chat about Phoebe going away has encouraged you to think you'll have a dash at Ian, you're wasting your time; no one has ever succeeded yet."

"What do you bet me that I get a couple of hours alone with him, before I leave?"

Tony jumped to his feet.

"Oh splendid! Let's take her on. Just the five of us, half-a-crown each. We'll bet you twelve-and-sixpence, Maimie, you never see the man alone at all."

Tania opened her mouth to protest, but Barbara

whispered:

"Don't worry. It's a hopeless task. We're bound to win."

But Tania was worried. She knew her Maimie.

CHAPTER 18

Maimie set about winning her bet in her usual direct manner. Every evening she came to the theatre, and hung about until she met Ian. On her first meeting she contented herself with planting in his mind the fact that she was in the town. On the second and third nights she tried to make him talk, but for all her charm only succeeded in dragging a few reluctant words from him. Discouraged, she almost faced the possibility of losing the bet. Then Tony's story of the white port came back to her. She bought a bottle, took it to the theatre, and while all the Company were on the stage, offered Brown a drink. One drink lead to two, two to a third; mellowed, Brown grew talkative. Maimie, who knew all she wanted to know about Phoebe, kept him off that topic, and encouraged him to talk of his master. By the time the curtain rang down on the act, there was a twinkle in her eye, and she looked even more assured than usual; she had a card, the only question was how best to play it.

Tania's attention was diverted from Maimie. She didn't care if she succeeded in vamping Ian, and quarrelling with Phoebe. For Tania, whose life had been all work, whose nursery-days had been non-existent, discovered that fairy-tales could come true. Her vague dreams had materialised, the unformed hopes in her mind had taken shape. Somebody was really doing those things she had dreamed of, but believed in her heart of hearts impossible. Somebody with very little money, and as unimportant as she was herself. Her cheeks flushed with excitement, and her eyes shining, she followed Amy Johnson's flight. Nothing that had happened in her life before, except Rose's death, had moved her so much, not even winning her car. She spent a small fortune on papers. What she liked best after reading the actual details of the flight were the chatty bits that proved that Amy Johnson was neither rich nor grand. Tania was forced to admit to herself that the other girl was better off than she was, for one thing she had a father who bought her a secondhand aeroplane. Still, in time, and by hard work, a secondhand aeroplane might be got without a father. She felt that if only Amy reached Australia, the day was not far off when she might do such a thing herself. Amy would have shown the world what could be done, and have given people like Nannie and "Young Mr. Bray" confidence in other women flyers, herself for instance. All day a prayer rang in her head—"Let her get there, let her get there, let her get there."

In the middle of the week Maimie told the girls and Tony that she intended winning her bet on the Friday. Although Phoebe had left on the previous Monday, leaving her husband in her children's charge, and in spite of the fact that they had seen Maimie talking to Ian, none of them believed she had a hope of winning.

"You haven't as much chance as a butter cat has in hell," said Tony, "but we'll all come to your rooms on

214

Friday, and I'll bring along some booze to celebrate your defeat. What time do you hope to do the ghastly deed?"

"In the afternoon."

" 'Off to my work,' said the little man to his big wife as he slipped down the bed." Tony turned with a grin to the others. "Excuse me being so common, but it slipped out all sudden like."

Friday afternoon found the five waiting for Maimie. They were expecting her by four, but at five o'clock she still hadn't appeared.

"She's a tryer and no mistake," said Beatrice. "I suppose she's still hanging round the hotel on the chance of bringing it off."

"I doubt it." Tony looked wise. "I don't believe Maimie would hang about for anybody, not even for a bet, would she, Tania?"

Tania, her mind in the clouds somewhere between Rangoon and Bangkok, looked vaguely at him. She hadn't heard the question, but was dimly aware she was being addressed.

"Oh, stop hopping off with Amy," said Tony, who together with the rest of the Company had discovered her furious interest in the flight. "I was asking about Maimie."

Tania was spared the effort of a reply, for Maimie strolled in. She held out her hand.

"Twelve-and-sixpence, chaps, and then I'm off."

"Good God!"

"You didn't really do it?"

"Tell us all about it."

Maimie took a tumbler of the promised drink.

"It was the white port again, Tony. I gave Brown three glasses. He said, 'Oh, Miss, 'e don't 'alf worry about his 'ealth. There isn't a remedy 'e don't try, from pillows of 'ops for not sleepin', to rollin' an iron ball up an' down 'is stummick for constipation. It don't matter to 'im if 'e's ill or not, 'ear of a cure an' 'e's bound to try it.' " She finished her imitation with the sniff that was a feature of the man. "Well," she went on, "that set the grey matter moving, and suddenly I had the bright idea. Chills! The next time I saw Ian I told him I had one. He was frightfully interested and recommended every foul cure under the sun. Then yesterday I said I was better, and did a bit of acting that left all you Shakespeareans at the post. I suddenly looked no end worried, turned on the sympathetic stuff, told him he wasn't looking too good, and asked if he didn't feel chillish himself. Of course directly I asked him that he began to wonder if he did, so I laid on the anxious-woman business good and thick, and then told him that I'd cured my chill with some marvellous dope that I had, and that if he'd stay in to-day covered with rugs and hot-water bottles, I'd send some of the stuff round to his hotel, and if he kept warm, drank the medicine, and trusted in the Lord, there was still hope. So this afternoon round I went to his hotel. They said they'd send up and see if he would see me, but they reckoned without little Maimie. 'Oh, he'll see me,' I said, 'he's expecting me,' and stepped into the lift."

Screams of "Go on" greeted this.

"I stayed the two hours, and then Phoebe blew in."

"Heavens!"

"What were you doing when she arrived?"

"What brought Phoebe back to-day?"

"I did," said Maimie calmly. "You don't suppose that I'm so hard-up for men that I spend a whole week scheming, and waste three-and-ninepence on white port, just to get two hours alone with one. Not this baby! I went to all that thought and expense to teach that plain cow of a wife of his not to look as though she'd bought the man with her spare cash, and to show her that it was still possible for him to look at someone else."

"But how did you get hold of her?" asked Beatrice.

"Those dear little children of hers; they don't know it, but they sent mummie a wire—'Please come, we are worried about daddy. Love, Viola and Sebastian.'"

They roared with laughter.

"But what were you doing when she came in?" asked Phyllis.

"Don't excite yourselves." Maimie held up her hand. "Believe me, the whole afternoon was as pure as the driven snow."

"That's as may be," said Tony. "What was the medicine?"

"Kruschen salts and water. I expect he'll be the better for it, he'll need that Kruschen feeling when Phoebe's done with him."

Barbara giggled.

"What did she say?"

"Ah!" Maimie paused expressively. "It's rather what she didn't say. She can say some foul things that woman when she's roused, and what a mind! There were Ian and I sitting miles away from each other, discussing his inside as pretty as pretty, but I shouldn't like to tell you what Phoebe suggested we'd been doing. Anyway, I've had enough of her and her tantrums; I'm going back to London to-night."

A chorus of surprised exclamations greeted this. Even Tania came back to earth. Maimie to be driven out of a town by another woman's tongue! It was incredible. She followed her into the bedroom when she went to pack her things.

"Why are you going? What did Phoebe say?"

"She knows something. Not much, but enough to make a lot of mischief. About me and George," she added casually.

"What the Lord? Oh goodness, I hoped you'd finished with him. Does Phoebe know him?"

"No, his wife. She saw her yesterday."

"I wonder how they came to talk about you."

"I wonder too. Anyway, I've got to see him." She packed feverishly.

Barbara came with Tania to see Maimie off. On the way back she offered a word of warning:

"Phoebe's a rotten person to get on the wrong side of."

Tania didn't hear her. She had bought an evening paper. "She's still safe," she remarked thankfully.

Phoebe's methods were subtle. It was no good

quarrelling with the younger sister because of the sins of the elder. But she wanted her to suffer nevertheless. Scarcely a performance but Tania was sent for by the stage-manager, he had received a complaint, he said. She hadn't been heard; the dancers were badly rehearsed, or her make-up was careless. Small complaints, but he hated to make them, for he knew her for a conscientious worker. The Company were indignant on her behalf. But complaints and sympathy alike were wasted on her, she lived in the air, only dragging herself back to earth while on stage, every other waking minute she spent with Amy Johnson. She was a nervous wreck on the Thursday, when no news of the flyer came through, and on the Saturday, when she heard of the safe arrival, she almost collapsed. She felt as tired as though she herself had gone through something; she could barely stand.

"She's done it," she whispered. "She's done it."

The next day being Sunday, there was the usual journey. Tania, a pile of papers beside her, settled down in her corner of the railway-carriage to enjoy article after article on the flight. She was so engrossed that she never noticed the other girls' interest in quite a different portion of the paper. Never noticed them having hurried conclaves with the rest of the Company in the corridor. Noticed nothing, in fact, until at the first stop Phoebe appeared at the carriage window. This was so amazing an event, that it even caught her attention.

"Well, Miss Whichart. Your sister seems to have

done it thoroughly this time." Phoebe's cheeks were shiny, and bright red with emotion. For over a week she had been at boiling-point. She had hardly slept or eaten. She could not bring herself to believe that nothing more had occurred between her husband and Maimie than a couple of hours' talk, sitting well apart in two armchairs. She had thought till her brain ached of some method of getting even with the girl. Chance had given her a bit of information, when Lady George Ronald had asked her if she happened to know a young actress called Maimie Whichart. Lady George had not explained why she asked, but when Phoebe had tried the name on Maimie, she had seen the girl start, and even in the midst of hysteria and temper had registered the fact, that here was a possible weapon. All the week she had twisted and turned her fragment of knowledge. Maimie knew Lord George Ronald. How well did she know him? How far had the affair gone? How much did Lady George know? Would it be possible to find out the whole business, and nip it in the bud by telling Lady George? She felt a fine woman when she reached this point, as she visualised herself disinterestedly saving a happy home. Meanwhile she could do nothing until she had another excuse to go to London. Doing nothing was foreign to her temperament, and kept her anger at white heat. Then this morning she had opened her paper, to find that fate had taken the whole business out of her hands. There it was in headlines. Lord George Ronald killed. Four o'clock in the morning, his car stationary, its lights out, a lorry had crashed into it, and Lord

George killed instantly. The other occupant of the car, Miss Maimie Whichart the actress, had miraculously escaped. Phoebe gloated over the details to an unresponsive Ian. "What a scandal! Her name will stink. Serve her right." Directly the train stopped, forgetful of her dignity, she hurried up the platform to see how hardly Tania had taken the news. She saw at a glance that the girl had no idea what had happened.

"Read that," she said, and shoved the paper into her hands.

Tania skimmed through the column.

"Oh, poor Maimie!" she said.

"Poor Maimie! Do you realise what you are saying? Do you know that man had a wife and children? Women like your sister are better dead."

Tania turned crimson. As usual words failed her. At last she stammered:

"You hateful woman! You to speak like that of Maimie. She's worth a million of you."

Never since her marriage had Phoebe been spoken to in such a manner. She completely lost control. She screamed, volumes of abuse and foul words showered from her. A frightened stage-manager ran for Ian. Knots of passengers and porters gathered round the carriage window. Tania got to her feet, and pulled her suitcase off the rack.

"Where are you going?" Barbara whispered. "Leave her alone, she'll go back to her carriage in a minute."

"I'm going home. I won't hear her talk about Maimie like that." She shook off Beatrice's restraining hand. "I'd have to go anyway, now, Maimie'll be wanting me."

By this time the stage-manager had returned bringing a reluctant Ian, who tried vaguely to soothe his wife, who paid no vestige of attention to him, but went on shouting insults at Tania and the absent Maimie. Tania pushed her way out of the carriage. The stage-manager asked her where she was going, and she replied firmly, "London." He tried to protest, but Phoebe drowned anything he had to say.

"Don't stop the little bitch. Let her go back to that precious sister of hers. We don't want any whores in this Company."

Barbara stayed behind when the Company's train left. She said she would follow later, somebody must see Tania safely off. She had enjoyed the whole fuss enormously. She had found Phoebe's descent from "The Grand Dame" very funny. As for Tania's share in the business, nothing would ever be more ludicrous. Tania, to whom scenes of any sort were so foreign, to be embroiled in such an exceedingly noisy and vulgar affair. Her championship of Maimie was the last glorious touch. Maimie so hopelessly in the wrong that you would have thought the most her family could have done was to invent some excuse for her. Yet, there was Tania, loyal in the face of hopeless odds, saying: "You hateful woman. You to speak like that of Maimie. She's worth a million of you."

"Oh Tania," she sighed, "I shall miss you. You and your family have kept me happy. Let me know how you get on, but don't imagine you are going home to either a heartbroken or a crushed and repentant Maimie. If she's upset she won't show it, and she doesn't know how to feel either crushed or repentant."

The train gave a whistle and a preliminary jerk.

"Good-bye," Tania struggled feverishly for adequate words. "I—I hope I'll see you some time."

"My goodness," Barbara called after her as the train began to move. "Losing your temper has made you quite chatty."

As the train went southwards, Tania sat in a dream. Events had moved too quickly for her. The mental chasm between the exalted mood into which Amy Johnson's flight had thrown her, and the sharp spasm of fury which had shaken her as she heard Maimie reviled, was too wide to be bridged in a few minutes. She felt rather as though she had been cut in half, one half still in the clouds, the other sitting in a third-class railway carriage, London-bound, still angry, but a little proud at having achieved a really decisive action. As the train reached the suburbs, she began to picture her reception at home. Maimie would be glad to see her, of that she was certain. Maimie would be terribly unhappy, and having an awful time, for Nannie would be being horrid, ashamed at the scandal, and Herbert would of course be furious, and refuse to see her again, most likely. Maimie, all her life so independent, would be glad of someone to back her up, someone to comfort her. At the vision of an unhappy and bullied Maimie, she tapped her foot on the floor. Oh, how slow the train was being!

She took the Underground to South Kensington. She found the walk from the station to the flat a weary drag carrying a suitcase, and as she pushed open the front door she thankfully rested it on the stairs. The flat door was open, she could hear voices. As she climbed upwards she recognised Mr. Higgs. He sounded annoyed.

"I tell you it's now or never. Either Daisy comes back with me to-night or she never comes into my house again. This trouble has fairly upset the wife, and no wonder, we've always been highly thought of in Surbiton."

"But Mr. Higgs," Herbert was speaking. "I gather your objection to Daisy remaining here is that she will be under the same roof as Maimie. I am suggesting that Maimie goes into an hotel to-night, and afterwards into a flat of her own. This scandal would never have occurred if I had had my way. I've always been fond of Maimie, months ago I wanted to give her a little place of her own. She's too high-spirited to be cooped up here. She hasn't enough to do, that's how all this business came about. But she wouldn't have it, said she must stay here, her salary was needed to keep the home together."

"Well," Mr. Higgs' voice boomed. "I don't know how that was, for Sunday after Sunday, Mrs. H. and I have said to Daisy, 'You and Nannie come and live here, you're our granddaughter, and here's your home when you like to come to it.'"

"And I told you," Daisy's voice chipped in, "that I couldn't. I'd promised Tania we'd all live together."

"That's right," Maimie was speaking, "and that's that. Do you want the kid to finish her tour, and find herself with no home?"

Tania crept down the stairs. She went out of the front door, and round the corner. There she leant against the wall. So that was it. Selfishly she had been tying the others to living in the flat. Nobody wanted it but her. Herbert wanted Maimie. Mr. Higgs wanted Daisy and Nannie. She mustn't stand in their way any more. But where should she go? And having found a place to go, how should she convince the others that she had given up the idea of wanting them to stick together? An enormous lump rose in her throat, it made every muscle ache. It would have helped her to cry. But tears never came easily to her, and she was incapable of crying in the street. She held her throat, it seemed to ache less that way. She must think. How should she explain her sudden arrival? It was impossible to explain that she had thought Maimie would be needing her, for if Maimie was hurt, she wasn't showing it, you could tell that from her voice. If she told the story of how she left the Company, what a fool she would feel! Looking back it did seem rather silly now. How annoyed Mr. Higgs and Herbert would be to see her! Such an awkward moment for her to turn up. Thinking of Mr. Higgs gave her an idea. Mr. Higgs was shocked at all that about Maimie in the paper. He wanted to get Daisy right away from it all. Why shouldn't she pretend to be shocked, pretend to want to get away from it too?

The argument was still going on as she climbed

the stairs once more. This time she walked into the flat. At her sudden arrival they were all silent. Impossible for Mr. Higgs to say: "What I say is this, why should Daisy consider Tania? She has her own life to lead——" which was what he had meant to say next. Impossible for Herbert to go on asking Maimie how much longer all their lives were to be upset to suit Tania, when there stood Tania in the doorway. Such a very white-faced Tania, that nobody felt like being unkind. After a pause Maimie said jauntily to hide the general embarrassment:

"Where have you sprung from?"

Tania opened her mouth. She was surprised to find that she had lost her voice, for only a whisper came:

"I've come for my things, I'm going away." Nobody spoke, so she went on, "You see, I read about you in the papers, Maimie, and I was—well, I thought—well, I'm not staying here any more."

She turned to go, but Daisy caught hold of her arm.

"You're not staying? I do think you're horrid, Tania. Maimie would have had a flat of her own months and months ago, only she wouldn't because she thought you were so keen on us all living together."

"What are you talkin' about, Tania?" Nannie broke in. "Where are you goin'?"

Tania shuffled her feet. "Now where am I going?" she thought desperately. Rose's words came to her: "Lock the Bibles away, unless things go very wrong."

226

Things couldn't well be more wrong than they were now.

"I'm going to my mother," she whispered.

Nannie opened her mouth to protest. Her mother might be dead, mightn't want her. Anyway, why wasn't she still on tour? But she swallowed her questions, for Tania had left the room.

In her bedroom Tania opened her suitcase and hurriedly stuffed in her Bible and her jeans. She heard a step outside, and saw Maimie's feet come in at the door. She glued her eyes on the carpet. She knew exactly what Maimie must be thinking of her. She hadn't the courage to look her in the face.

"You poor cow," said Maimie. "Did you really think you'd get away with that stuff on me? I suppose you overheard what those men were saying. As it turns out, this is the best thing that could happen to you. All this hanging about with me and Daisy won't get you anywhere. You'd never have made a move on your own, but now it's forced on you. Get out, go and look for that mother of yours. If she's dead, we've got another think coming, but if she's alive she's got to help you. You'll never do a damn bit of good on the stage. If she can't give you a home, she'll probably make you an allowance, and then you can fiddle about with machinery till you're black in the face."

The sudden knowledge that Maimie understood, and didn't hate her for what she had said, made her coming separation from the only background she knew even more deplorable. She felt she couldn't stand much more. She picked up her suitcase.

"Good-bye," she whispered.

"Why do you keep whispering?" asked Maimie crossly, who found it aggravatingly pathetic.

"I can't help it," Tania explained. "I've suddenly lost my voice."

Maimie looked at her shrewdly.

"You take life too hard, old girl. You simply ask to get hurt. Nothing could be more lousy than what's happened to me, but I'll be damned before I'll let it get me down."

Tania turned to go.

"Keep Daisy and Nannie in the sitting-room," she pleaded. "I'd rather see myself off, and Nannie will be full of fuss."

Maimie nodded. Not for worlds would she have let Tania see that there were tears in her eyes.

CHAPTER 19

Alfy and Mrs. Alfy were having their evening meal; high tea with kippers as a relish.

" 'ark, Alfy," said Mrs. Alfy, "give over drinkin' a minute, I want to listen. I thought I 'eard a knock."

Alfy obediently "gave over". Yes, there was a feeble knocking. He crossed to the door. Tania stood on the doorstep. Repressed emotion had stiffened her muscles. Her face felt like a board. With a struggle she forced a smile, as still whispering, she explained she had come for her car.

"Goin' out in 'er now?" questioned Alfy in surprise. "Why, you 'aven't——" he stopped suddenly with his mouth open, for Mrs. Alfy was making terrifying faces at him, intended to show that in her opinion something was wrong, and if so, it was a woman's job, and that the best thing he could do was to keep his mouth shut.

Mrs. Alfy pulled a chair up to the fire, and almost forced Tania into it.

"Well, there now, if we aren't pleased to see you," she said comfortably, "and just in time for a nice cupatea." She poured a cup of remarkable strength. "There, you drink that, for all of it's May, these nights are that parky, they freeze your marrer."

Tania looked drearily at the cup in her hand. She didn't want it. She felt vaguely sick, but the fire was nice and warm on her legs, and Mrs. Alfy's chatter had the same soothing effect as listening to Miss Poll. She took a sip of the tea. It seemed to relax her muscles. But as they relaxed, her control weakened. To her horror she began to cry. Not just a tear or two trickling down her nose, which she might have passed off as a cold, but loud gasping sobs, which shook her whole body, and which she was quite powerless to prevent.

Alfy stared at her with his mouth open, until his wife asked him severely if he was, or was not going out on that job. Surprised, he enquired, "What job?" whereupon, if looks could have killed, he received one which should have prevented his ever leaving the door, followed by a series of jerks and nods, which meant, even to his mind, unskilled in such semaphorish talk, that in Mrs. Alfy's opinion the place for him was the street.

Mrs. Alfy was a woman of tact. She had, as she had always told her husband, "taken a rare fancy" to Tania. She had seen quite a lot of her while she had worked in the garage, enough to realise how reserved the girl was, and how unlike her this unrestrained crying. She said nothing, but quietly piled together the tea things, noting mentally that a good cry would do a power of good. After a time Tania's sobs grew quieter. Then they stopped. She raised a ravaged and exhausted face.

"I'm so terribly sorry," she gasped.

"Don't you mind me, dearie. You let me make you a nice fresh cupatea, that cup's not as 'ot as it was. A good cry never did anyone any 'arm yet. Many's the time when I've felt all-over like, an' snappin' at Alfy fit to beat the band, I've said to myself, 'What you need my girl's a good cry.' Believe me, or believe me not, down I've plumped in that very chair, 'ad me cry out, an' felt a sight better for it." While she had been talking she had cut and spread some bread-and-butter. She handed it to Tania. "What time did you 'ave your dinner?"

Tania thought back to lunch time. Dinner? Had she had any, and if so, where? She remembered coffee and a biscuit with Barbara, but nothing more. Sheepishly she explained that she had been travelling and had had no time for real dinner.

"So I should say!" Mrs. Alfy pretended to sound cross. "No wonder you look as cheap as a 'errin' on a Monday, an' no more voice than a 'ap'orth of chewin'-gum. You ought to be ashamed of yourself, a great girl of your age, no more sense than a baby. You eat that bread-and-butter while I boils you a couple of eggs."

Tania would have protested, but she was silenced by an indignant sniff. So she meekly nibbled her bread-and-butter, and found to her amazement that it didn't make her sick, in fact she felt hungry.

"Was you thinkin' of takin' that car of yours out for a turn?" Mrs. Alfy asked casually, as she put a saucepan on the fire.

"Not a turn exactly, you see I'm goin' away to-night."

"Oh, where was you garagin' it?"

"Well, somewhere on the road. I want to have a look at a map if Alfy will lend me one."

"Goin' far?" Mrs. Alfy questioned even more casually.

"Cumberland."

Mrs. Alfy showed no surprise.

"Do you like your eggs done 'ard or soft?" she asked.

The eggs boiled, and placed in two pink and gold egg-cups, with "A Present from Broadstairs" written across them, were put on a tray on Tania's knees.

"Now I'll 'ave to leave you for a minute or two, dearie. I 'ave to go to the 'Cow and Dragon' to fetch Alfy's pint. An' let me find every scrap of them eggs finished when I come back."

In the bar of the 'Cow and Dragon' Alfy was having a drink. His wife hurried in, she drew him to one side.

"Now just you listen 'ere, Alfy Bristowe——"

A few minutes later Alfy unwillingly left the bar. He had been given a job requiring tact, a quality which he had been told repeatedly throughout his married life he failed to possess. Anxiously he entered his kitchen, sheepishly he smiled at Tania. " 'ad a good tea?" he asked mournfully.

Tania nodded. Her throat still ached too acutely to make talking pleasant. Alfy nervously cleared his throat.

"Look 'ere, Tania, you said when you come in as 'ow you'd come for your car. Well, mother says—well, what I meant to say is" he corrected hurriedly, "as it ain't 'ere, leastways, not to-night, not till to-morrow morning."

"Why, where is it?" Tania's whisper sounded

surprised.

Shifting in agony from one foot to the other, for an inventive tongue was not one of his gifts, Alfy plunged into his story:

"You see, it's this way. I was tellin' the men down at the garridge 'ow well your car ran, an' Nobby—you remember Nobby Clark? 'im with the ginger 'air—'e says to me as 'ow 'e'd like to take 'er out, so I says as 'ow 'e could, as I was sure you wouldn't mind, an'—well, that's where she is," he finished lamely.

Tania smiled at him forlornly. She was wondering where she would spend the night, she had intended sleeping in her car somewhere on the road. If she had not been so tired and dazed, it would have struck her how odd it was that Alfy, the most punctilious person with other people's cars, should have so far changed his spots as to lend out hers. But intent on the problem of where to sleep, she noticed nothing. She supposed that as she was not getting her car that night, she ought to be going, perhaps when she got outside she would get an inspiration as to where to sleep. She got to her feet.

"Good-bye, Alfy, I'll be round for the car in the morning." She turned to the door. "Please thank Mrs. Alfy for my tea." Alfy gazed at her distractedly. This wasn't what ought to happen. His orders had been to tell her he had lent her car out to Nobby. As if he would lend out her car, and anyway Nobby had the influenza. But the point had been that Tania was to be kept for the night, and here she was going before his wife came back. He was spared the worst dressing-down of his life, because Mrs. Alfy ran into Tania on the doorstep.

"What! Goin'?" she demanded, casting an indignant look at the cringing Alfy.

Tania explained about her car. Mrs. Alfy turned in apparent rage to Alfy, and told him he ought to be ashamed of himself, making free with Tania's car like that. Tania assured her it was quite all right and again turned to go. But Mrs. Alfy's stout form was in the doorway.

"Now look 'ere," she said, "if you wants to start first thing, the best thing you can do is to sleep 'ere. They can't be expectin' you at 'ome as you meant to start to-night. Not 'avin' your car is Alfy's fault, so if you don't mind a sofa, you can sleep 'ere an' welcome." Tania was too thankful to protest, so she went on—"An' Alfy can get 'is map out an' show you the road. Cumberland she's goin' to, Alfy."

"Near Carlisle," Tania amended.

Alfy turned to a bookshelf and took down a bundle of maps and guides. A gleam of happiness lighted Tania's eyes. Mrs. Alfy looked at her with approval.

"That's right, Alfy," she said, turning to her husband. "You draw a chair up next to Tania's an' you can 'ave a look together."

Alfy bent over the map. He traced the road with a dirty finger-nail:

"Then you get on the Great North Road," he said.

Suddenly like frost before the first rays of sun, Tania's misery began to melt:

"Alfy," she whispered, "what can she do?"

When Tania had been sent to sleep on the sofa in the parlour, Mrs. Alfy came back into the kitchen. She sat down by the kitchen table, and solemnly shook her head:

"I don't like it, Alfy. What's this goin' to that Carlisle mean? Is she safe in that car of 'ers? Never been in it, 'as she?"

"Tania's as safe in any car ever made, seems to understand them like. Funny in a girl."

" 'ow far is this Carlisle?"

Alfy studied the map, and made some laborious calculations on the margin:

"More'n three hundred miles," he said at last.

"An' 'ow much petrol is that goin' to use?"

Alfy, with a much furrowed forehead, and with loud suckings at his pencil, settled down to further calculations. After great labour he announced that in his opinion she would use all of twelve gallons.

"An' 'ow much will that cost in money?"

Alfy groaned.

"Oh come off it," he protested. "Want to give me the 'eadache?"

"Oh get on with you," replied his wife firmly, "don't act so stupid. 'ow are we to know 'ow much money she ought to 'ave, if we don't know 'ow much she's goin' to need."

"What's 'er money got to do with us?"

"That's right," Mrs. Alfy complained, "that's right. Go on, ask some more silly questions instead of addin'."

Gloomily Alfy returned to his calculations, and at

last after much suckings and mutterings decided that it would work out as near as a spit to a pound.

Mrs. Alfy got to her feet, and raked out the ashes.

"Well, now you worked that out, we can go to bed. It passes me 'ow you don't get cheated down the garridge, with you so slow at figurin'."

Tania spent a miserable night. For one thing, the horsehair sofa in the parlour was far from being an ideal bed. Slippery to start with, it had as well a bad list, only by careful balancing was it possible to prevent yourself from sliding on to the floor. In the ordinary way she would not have minded this in the least, for she could sleep on anything, but to-night she only slept in short snatches, awaking with a start to find herself moaning and crying, and the sudden jump of her awakening invariably pitching her on to the floor. By two o'clock she had decided it wasn't good enough, so she sat upright, determined to stay awake. Two o'clock in the morning is a bad hour even to the most contented people with a good day both behind and before them. To the unhappy and anxious, it's terrifying. The thoughts that can at least be kept at arm's length in the reasonable daylight, in the night hours settle on the mind like vultures on a dead body. Gone for Tania was any pleasure in her car, or excitement at the journey before her, and nothing remained but the stark bleak fact that their home was broken up for ever, and she was the only one who cared. Daisy was sunk irretrievably into the arms of Surbiton, and Maimie into the arms of Herbert. Maimie would of course emerge from Herbert's arms, but it was impossible to pretend she would ever want to live at home again. Even Nannie was gone. What was going to happen to her? Would her mother want her? It was most unlikely. She unpacked her Bible and stared at the flyleaf—"To my baby"—signed "Tania Lissen," and the address in Cumberland and the date. Nearly seventeen years ago, and in all that time no interest taken in her, no effort made to see her, not even a little money sent to educate her. Maimie was mad to suppose such a mother would want her, or do anything for her. Looked at now, the whole idea of the trip to Carlisle appeared fantastic. "I was silly ever to think of it," she said out loud. She shut the Bible and tossed it back into the empty suitcase. "Then if not to Carlisle, where am I going?" she said to herself, and suddenly remembered Alfy's letter—"I have a business proposition to put before you." Of course that was what she must do, she must talk it over with Alfy. He would probably give her a job in his garage, and he might use her car as a taxi, and if she wasn't worth wages just at first, perhaps they would keep her and feed her. Then a picture of Maimie came suddenly before her. Maimie had been so keen she should try and find her mother. "Oh Maimie, Maimie," she whispered. The ache in her throat was coming back worse than ever. She gripped her pyjama coat tightly across her with both hands, there seemed less room to be miserable in it while it was held like that. Sobs shook her, she rolled into a ball and buried herself in the unconsoling horsehair of the sofa, where somehow she must have become wedged, for she went to sleep.

CHAPTER 20

Tania awoke to find a rather feeble sun struggling through the Nottingham lace blinds. Mrs. Alfy came in with a cup of tea.

"Good mornin', dear. It's 'ardly seven o'clock, but I thought you'd be wantin' to make an early start seein' as you've all that way to go. I've brought you a nice cupatea, an' by the time you're dressed an've 'ad a bit of a wash, an've put your traps together, I'll 'ave your breakfast waitin'."

When Tania arrived in the kitchen Alfy had finished eating:

"I'm goin' on down to the garridge," he said. "I'll 'ave a look over your car, you come along down as soon as you've finished."

Tania, much to Mrs. Alfy's disgust, scrambled through her breakfast, for she was in a hurry to have her talk with Alfy. Maimie or no Maimie, she could not help feeling that if only she could persuade Alfy to take her on, a nice steady job in the garage was worth a dozen mothers.

She arrived at the garage to find her car being filled with water and petrol. It was a grey and scarlet Morris coupé. She had forgotten how exquisite she was. She stood in front of her spellbound, trying to believe that such speed and elegance were really hers.

"Looks a bit of all right, doesn't she?" said Alfy, appreciating her abstraction.

His remark brought her back to earth.

"Alfy, in your letter to me you said you had a business proposition to talk to me about. What was it?"

Alfy scratched his head.

"I'm glad you brought that up, Tania, for I've been feelin' badly about it, very badly I 'ave, seein' as you might 'ave counted on it like. You see, it was this way. When I wrote to you, I thought as maybe you'd like me to garridge your car, an' pay her licence an' all that, an' use 'er for a bit of taxi work. Then odd times when you was free, there she'd be for you to take for a run."

"Yes," said Tania eagerly, "and me to drive her when she was being a taxi?"

"No. Oh no." Alfy sounded injured. "Taxi work ain't a woman's job. I always tole you there was no work for a woman in this line. No, what I thought was, that if I was to use the car like that you wouldn't 'ave to sell 'er, an' there she'd be for you to drive into the country an' that of a Sunday."

Tania said nothing. Her eyes, looking into his, were tragic and very black. Embarrassed, he hurried on:

"But now it's this way. Times is that bad I can't manage to run an extra car. This last month I 'aven't picked up enough work to keep one on the road, let alone two. The city gents what comes back of an evening, used to take a taxi regular, but now they walks or goes on a bus, it's fair sickening to see 'em. They says times is bad, but it's my belief that sort don't know what bad times is, it's us of the proletariat what knows that."

Tania didn't answer. She was thinking that this settled it. Now she had no alternative, she must try and find her mother. She looked at Alfy, she ought to say something, but her outlook appeared so utterly gloomy it crushed her. To add to her depression it began to drizzle.

Alfy gazed at the sky, and shook his head:

"Dirty," he muttered, "very dirty."

He came back with her when she went back to the house to pick up her suitcase. He wanted to see how she drove the new car. His only criticism was that she drove too fast.

"Silly it is, downright silly. Some poor fool that can't drive will run into you one day, an' then where'll you be? Down Queer Street I shouldn't wonder."

"I'm sorry," Tania apologised, "but it does seem so mean to hold her in, when I can feel her simply bursting to go all out."

Mrs. Alfy was on the doorstep when they arrived. She drew Tania into the parlour:

" 'ow much money 'ave you, dear?"

Tania flushed:

"Two pounds, three shillings, and fourpence halfpenny."

"Well, 'ere's another pound what I'm lendin' you, I don't like you to start short."

A tremendous argument followed. In the end, Tania, against her will, was forced to take ten shillings. Remembering that Alfy had owned that times were bad, she was only persuaded to take that much after

Mrs. Alfy had pointed out that if all else failed she could sell her car to pay the debt.

Both the Alfys stood on the doorstep as she drove off:

"Mind you comes to see us the minute you're back," Mrs. Alfy called after her. Tania nodded, put her foot on the accelerator, and vanished round the corner.

In spite of the drizzle, and her most uncertain future, by the time she reached Barnet she was singing. It was impossible to keep a heavy heart while the car purred beneath her, and the miles flicked away behind her. She missed the thrill she had expected on the Great North Road, for she was some miles up it before she realised she was on it at all. She careered, singing at the top of her voice, through Biggleswade and Stamford, and dashed on to Newark, where the rain had ceased to be a drizzle, and had become a steady downpour, but quite undaunted, and singing louder than ever, she sped on to Doncaster, and there stopped, suddenly realising that she was enormously hungry. A quick calculation showed her that two pounds, thirteen and fourpence halfpenny, large sum though it was, would have to be handled carefully, if, as seemed probable, her mother didn't want her and she had to come straight back. While her car was being attended to, she wandered down the road looking for food that was both cheap and filling. She ended by buying six doughnuts, remembering that she had felt extraordinarily fat on an occasion when she had eaten three. "How gloriously fat I shall feel," she thought, "after I've eaten six." She also bought herself an orange by way of a drink. As she paid the man at the petrol pump she thought with a sigh how much more expensive a car was to feed than a girl. On the other side of Doncaster she got out for a stretch, and to eat her buns. She was surprised to find that she could only manage five of them, they seemed amazingly filling, so she laid the last one on the back seat for her tea. Fortified she drove on. The rain had stopped, but masses of lowering grey clouds hung in the sky. The hilly road to Wetherby needed her attention, but she was singing again by the time she reached Bowes, where she paused for a cup of tea, and to eat her last bun. As she drove into Penrith the sun was sinking westwards in a glory of black and crimson clouds. She looked at the signpost, 'Carlisle, 18 miles'. She drew a deep breath and slowed down. On enquiry she learned that her destination was through Carlisle and out the other side. She found the house quite easily, but was appalled at its size; her mother must be very rich, she thought, to live in a house like that. She hadn't the courage to go to the front door, but there was a lodge, and at this she knocked timidly. A sad-faced woman came to the door with a baby on her arm, by her accent Tania knew she was from across the Border, as in answer to her enquiry for Miss Lissen, she said:

"Would it be the young leddy, or the auld one?"

Tania was flummoxed:

"I don't know," she said vaguely.

"Weel, there's Miss Grace, the auld Maister's

sister, and there's Miss Tania, the auld Maister's daughter."

"It's Miss Tania I want."

"Weel, they're no livin' here the noo. If you'll bide a wee I'll gie ye Miss Grace's address. As for Miss Tania it would be hard to say where she'd be, for she's aye stravaiging." The woman went into the lodge and came back with an envelope. "Here's the address. Miss Grace aye gies it me when she's from hame."

Tania took the envelope. Her heart stood still, for she saw the word "Sussex". The envelope faded as her memory swept her backwards, and she saw instead the grey-green striped downs, and felt in retrospect the glory of space. She thanked the woman, put the envelope in her pocket, and jumped into her car— "Sussex," she whispered as she touched the self-starter. "Sussex."

She needed the spur of being Sussex-bound, for she was deadly tired, and rather anxious about her money. Would it hold out, she wondered? If she ate almost nothing could she do it? What was she going to do if her mother wasn't in Sussex? The woman had only said Miss Grace was there. As "The Auld Maister" presumably meant her grandfather, the Auld Maister's sister would be her great-aunt. Did great-aunts count as great-aunts when they were illegitimate? Anyway this one must be a very, very old lady; after all, she was her mother's aunt, and a mother couldn't be very young. Surely she must find her mother in Sussex? Surely the two old ladies would live together? Hopefully she visualised two figures by a fireside, for the expression "aye stravaiging" had meant nothing to her.

She stopped at Penrith to feed herself, and fill up the car. She couldn't face any more doughnuts, filling though they had undoubtedly proved to be, so she purchased half a pound of ginger nuts, and, wasting no time, ate them as she drove along. She planned to drive until she could drive no more, and then to pull up in a field or by the side of the road, for a little sleep, provided she could find a sufficiently isolated spot where the police were not likely to see her, for she was painfully conscious that she was driving without a licence, and wouldn't be old enough to have one until next month. It was lucky, she thought, the Alfys hadn't known her age, or they would never have let her start.

The towns and villages through which she had dashed earlier in the day now appeared vaguely as a flurry of lights. She no longer sang, she needed all the energy she had left to drive at all. On she careered, going steadily south but frequently losing her road in the darkness, and fumbling for signposts to set her right. In the early morning when she should have been arriving at Doncaster, she found herself in a narrow lane. Where or when she had gone wrong she had no idea. It seemed to her hours since she had last seen a signpost. She got out to prospect. Her legs were so stiff that they almost gave way under her. She found, away from the safe shelter of her car, the country appallingly black and lonely, and apparently inhabited with queer beasts, for there were the most mysterious and terrifying noises. With her heart in her mouth she crept along, and a few yards further on found a widening in the lane where it seemed safe to park. With some manœuvring she got her car there, turned off the lights, and with no thought of the police, rolled herself into a ball on the back seat and promptly fell asleep.

She was wakened by a cheerful "Whoa there!" Sitting up, she found herself looking into a farm. Leaning over the gate she asked the farm hand who had wakened her, where she was, and which was the road to London. He appeared to be half-witted, for he simply stood and stared at her, but when she repeated her question for the third time, he vanished into the farm and reappeared with a woman, who not only directed her carefully, but on hearing she had been lost and had slept the night in her car, insisted on her coming into the farm, and gave her tea and bread and butter, and refused to be paid for it. Warmed and heartened by this bit of good fortune, Tania took to the road again in grand spirits.

It was nearly one o'clock before she reached London. As she crossed to the south side of the Thames, tired though she was, her heart sang. To be going back to Sussex, driving her own car, it seemed too good to be true. She couldn't drive fast enough to satisfy the urge that was in her to see the downs again.

It was late in the afternoon before she saw them, and at their first glimpse she clapped on her brakes, regardless of the furious words of a driver behind her to whom she had given no indication that she intended to stop. The downs hadn't changed. There they were with their patches and stripes, and racing shadows, exactly as she had left them seven years ago. It had never struck her that there might be no downlands in the part of Sussex for which she was heading. The address said "Near Arundel, Sussex." She had never been to Arundel, but the 'Sussex' was enough for her; if in Sussex at all, then there must be downs. Having soothed her soul with a long stare she set off again, and outside Arundel she was directed to a winding lane, and was told she would find the house she wanted on the side of the hill. Her car climbed steadily upward, and suddenly round a bend she came to a white gate. The house lay some way back, it looked square and contented, with a cheerful front garden full of flowers. Unpacking her Bible, but leaving her suitcase in the car, she climbed out and opened the gate. She was so tired and hungry that the short walk up to the house seemed treble its length. The front door stood wide open, she couldn't see a bell so she knocked. A tall gaunt woman appeared, dressed in a tweed coat and skirt, with an appallingly ugly felt hat precariously balanced on her thin grey hair. Tania smiled at this apparition, secretly hoping that this was not her mother. Surely her mother couldn't look quite like that?

"Are you Miss Tania Lissen?" she asked nervously.

"No, I'm Miss Lissen. My niece has gone to meet you. I'm very glad to see you, for what we were going to do with the poor things if you hadn't come, I don't know, for one book says one thing and one another, and there are all those sacks of food, and whether the poor creatures like them all mixed together or served as separate courses, I have really no idea, and the books don't seem to say, but now you are here I can safely leave them to you. Come along, I expect you are eager to see them, for I understand that people like you, who spend your whole lives with them, get quite fond of them, which I confess amazes me, for to my mind they seem not only stupid, but not quite nice, but maybe that's my ignorance, and if we stay here long enough, which is most unlikely as my niece seldom stays anywhere for more than a day or two, I might get to understand them." She stopped suddenly, for Tania, already exhausted to dropping point, was listening to this flow of apparently meaningless words with the most vacant stare. "Oh dear," Miss Lissen went on, "I do hope, my child, that you are brighter than you look, for we need all your intelligence. All," she emphasised, as she led the way through the hall and out of a door on the other side of the house. She pointed to a field in front of them, dotted with white objects. "There they are," she said.

Tania now realised that all this conversation had been about chickens. To her eyes, seeing almost double with fatigue, there seemed to be all the chickens in the world gathered before them. She was not allowed long to look at them, for she was hurried across to a shed, which was full of sacks, boxes, empty bowls, bowls of repulsive-looking leavings, bowls of crusts, weighing machines, tins of mustard, measuring glasses, wooden spoons, and jugs.

"There!" said Miss Lissen triumphantly. "I really think you must find all you want, for I've bought everything the books mentioned, including those recommended for when the poor creatures are broody, which I trust none of them are, for it sounds a most distressing complaint, and the treatment seems most unpleasant, and I've bought some tins of mustard, for one of the books stated that it was a good thing to put inside the eggs if the birds should take to eating them, but really I don't mind if they do eat a few, for we can easily spare them."

Still chattering, she wandered away, leaving Tania staring despairingly at the mass of chicken impediments before her. She went to the door and looked at the birds. They seemed a long way off—"I'll feed the nearest ones first," she said to herself. Feeling quite incapable of feeding even the handiest of chickens before she herself had had something to eat, she chose one of the least stale crusts out of the basins, and furtively, with her eyes on the door, bolted it down. Slightly revived, she poured portions out of most of the bags into the bowls of refuse and bread, and nervously started out. She had never known chickens on this sort of personal footing before, in fact she'd scarcely ever met one face to face, and to her horror, at the sight of her, these charged at her, looking at her most unpleasantly, she thought. She wondered if they always looked like that, or whether it was because they had seen her eating their bread. She couldn't find any clean plates on which to serve their food, the various dishes standing about looked very dirty, and she was far too afraid of the birds to hunt about, so she popped the bowl of food on the ground, and retreating from the pushing and struggling that ensued, went back to the shed for more. As she was stirring up another bowlful, she heard voices outside— a deep, rather lovely voice called:

"Aunt Grace, here she is. Here's Miss Jones."

"Rubbish! that's not Miss Jones. Miss Jones is in the shed."

"What?" Quick, light steps sounded outside, and turning, Tania saw her mother framed in the doorway.

CHAPTER 21

In all her dreams she had never imagined that her mother would look like this. So vivid, so lovely, so young. Incredibly far though she was removed from the old lady by the fireside that she had pictured, she knew at once who she was. The figure in the doorway spoke:

"I think there's been some mistake. My aunt says——"

Turning, Tania picked up her Bible from the shelf behind her, and held it out. Her mother didn't take it, for even as she had picked it up, Tania saw her recognise it, and realise who she must be. All the colour drained from her cheeks. She swayed slightly.

"It's all right," said Tania, her voice gruff with pity. "Don't worry, I only came to look you up. I'm going now."

Her mother put a restraining arm round her shoulders, then hurriedly withdrew it, ashamed of so eager a gesture:

"Don't go," she said, "I'm too terribly—oh too terribly——" she fumbled round for expressive words.

Her daughter grinned. Here was someone as tongue-tied as herself. With the grin they established a wordless understanding.

Lolling against the sacks of chicken food they talked. Tania gave a skeleton portrait of her life. A very bare history, with all her feelings left out. Giving no reason for her sudden appearance, she finished up by saying:

"So I went to look for you in that house of yours up by Carlisle, and there they gave me this address, so I came down here."

"But did you start looking for me yesterday morning?" her mother asked. Tania nodded. "Why, you must have driven simply miles then. How too dreadfully exhausting. It's the world's bore, but you ought to go to bed at once."

Tania tried to protest, but she couldn't hide the fact that she could hardly stand, though privately she put this down in part to a diet of doughnuts and biscuits. Her mother ordered a bath to be turned on for her, sent for her suitcase and promised to see her car safely garaged. All this was very pleasant, but hunger was gnawing at her vitals. "What's the betting," she said to herself, "that she thinks I'd rather have something light, and gives me milk and biscuits for my supper?" However, she was no sooner in bed than her dinner appeared on a tray, a large and substantial dinner of which she ate every morsel. As she swallowed her last mouthful, she lolled forward almost blind with sleep. She was just conscious that her mother appeared to say good-night, but she was only capable of a grunt in response.

She awoke to find the sun shining, and was startled to see it was nearly twelve o'clock. She leaped across to the window, and drew back the chintz curtains. Her windows faced the chickens, with Miss

Jones's back bent in toil among them, but her eyes skipped quickly over the near view, to gloat on a most heavenly stretch of downs. Gazing entranced, a glorious thought came to her. Perhaps her mother would let her stay here, and since she seemed very rich, would let her learn to fly. It would be an investment, for she could learn sky-writing, all that sort of thing. She could go in her car every morning to a flying-school, and come back and sleep here at night. No more moving about on tour. Her own car to drive in. Working hard for her ground licence, really understanding aeroplanes. Perhaps Maimie, and Daisy, and Nannie, coming to stay. The whole vision made her gasp, it was too perfect.

She was recalled from her dreams by her mother, who came in to say that she had seen she was awake, that it was too late for breakfast, but there was some tea coming for her:

"Would you be too tired," she asked, "to drive us, you and me, up to town this afternoon? I thought we might stay there a couple of days, and then go on to Paris to get you some clothes, and then I rather thought we might go to Java."

"Java?" Tania was startled. She had dimly heard of Java, because Amy Johnson had flown over it. But when one could stop in Sussex why go to Java, she wondered, unless of course one was flying there. "Fly there, do you mean?" she asked.

"Fly! My gracious me, no. On a boat, you know. It's the wrong time of year of course, but I don't mind the heat, and I don't suppose you will."

Tania didn't answer. She was thinking what a pity it was that she was the only person in the world who liked having a home. The tea came in. Throwing her mind on to food made her think of the chickens:

"We couldn't leave all those chickens, could we?" she asked hopefully.

"Why not? There's Miss Jones. Anyway, neither Aunt Grace nor I have taken to them. I bought the place with them two days ago. I thought they'd be fun. They aren't much."

"Will Miss Lissen come to Java, too?"

"You can't very well call her Miss Lissen, you know. Could you bear to call her Aunt Grace? No, she won't come with us, she's sick of travelling. When I told her about you last night she said, 'Thank goodness, that means I can settle down.' She's travelled round and round the world with me, you know."

Tania, completely shattered by this vision of herself and her mother travelling for ever, could think of nothing to say, so she took refuge in her teacup.

"Talking of names," her mother went on, "I know it's a disgusting bore for you, but you'll have to call me something. Mother is too fantastic, and we can't both be Tania."

Tania nodded, appreciating the unnamed difficulties.

"Did my father ever call you anything besides Tania?" she asked.

"Well, he called me Mendelssohn sometimes."

"Mendelssohn! Why?"

"He said I was a song without words. It was a

joke, you know."

Tania, marvelling at the sentimentality of "those old days" as she mentally stigmatised her mother's girlhood, decided it was as good a name as any other, and no one but themselves would ever know of its origin.

"Right. I'll call you Mendelssohn," she agreed.

Mother and daughter drove to town that afternoon. Tania slightly consoled for turning her back on Sussex by the knowledge that a telegram had been despatched to Nannie, asking her to bring Daisy to lunch the next day, and a prepaid one to Herbert asking for Maimie's address.

London, seen from the angle of Brown's hotel, was an entirely different place from the London she had always known, and Maimie, Daisy, and Nannie seemed at first quite different people when they were being visitors. But after lunch her mother took Nannie off to her bedroom for a talk, and the sisters were left alone. Sitting together on a sofa, their heads touching, they stopped being different and became themselves. In spite of the fact that they had all met the previous Sunday, they had an immense amount to tell each other. Maimie, contrary to her usual custom, was the most reticent, Tania didn't think she looked happy. Daisy, secure in Surbiton, the cherished, brilliant grandchild, was radiant. Whatever Tania might feel about herself, her sisters were enchanted at her good fortune.

They took the Dover boat express two days later. Maimie, Daisy, and Nannie saw them off.

"See that she wears something warm in those foreign parts, Mum," said Nannie. "She turns livery that easy."

"Good-bye, Tania," said Daisy, with the tears dripping off her nose. Maimie slapped her on the back, and said nothing.

With her heart in her eyes Tania watched them, till the train turned round a bend.

"You'll miss the others, I'm afraid," said her mother sympathetically.

"Oh, I don't know. I shan't see much of Daisy now, I suppose, but when we're home we shall always have Maimie with us more or less. Herbert's not a bit permanent, you know."

"No, I suppose not," agreed her mother doubtfully. "I do hope you'll like travelling, Tania," she said after a pause. "I want to take you about, and show you the world, and perhaps later on find you a husband."

"I'd rather have an aeroplane," exclaimed Tania, horrified out of her usual reticence.

"Would you? Do you want to fly? Well, could you bear to try travelling for a year first, and after that you can do what you like. I think you'll find Java fun, you know. The people are too attractive, and they have——"

But Tania wasn't listening. Her mind was on the skyline, where an aeroplane, like some giant silver bird, was darting towards them.